Hidden Allies, False Friends

Book 2 in the Varthien Saga

Other works by this author

Dragon Silver, Wizard Gold (Book 1 of The Varthien Saga)

As Kristine Sihto

Life Wires

Hidden Allies, False Friends

Kris Sihto

Kris Sihto

2025

First Printing: 2025

Paperback ISBN 978-0-9942984-1-6
eBook ISBN 978-0-9942984-2-3

Cover Art *Archaeidae sapiens* ©2024 Kris Sihto

Contents

ATINIEN MOUNTAIN
ARNEDIA
ARNEDIA
YURDELT
THENTON
ARAC
NORTHEASTERN REACHES
SHARD SEA
COUNCIL ISLE
BAKAR
PUGTON
NOCK
LIBBET
CERINOT
MARTHUNE
MERETHIEN
VENT
TERRIL SEA
HOOD'S SEA
FIGELIS
DOUB CIRCLE RANGE
LANRASH
ARNEDIA
KARASTA
SHARPSTONE
WAMANIL
SARDENNE
PERU QOTH
TITINGAARD
GARTHANIAN FOREST
TO DELINGAARD
N
PAVANE
TO JERROS

Acknowledgements

I would like to acknowledge Jessica for her counsel. The situations with Norman were hard to nut through and her opinion was greatly sought after.

My father, as always, has been steadfast in his commentary, often being the first to see my raw drafts.

Des, your questions always make me look deeper into what needs explaining. Thank you.

Finally, to Bull and Aston, thank you for the words about the first book. They've given me the encouragement to try to make each book better than before.

What has come before

An accident caused the death of a young mage by the name of Gareth Diefen on the day that his son, Peter, was born. It was unfortunate that his friend, Norman Linter, had been part of that accident, as Norman went on to carry that guilt, retreating to an isolated tower in the woods.

Ten years later, Peter discovered a wyrmling (Petunia) in the mud, and Norman happened to be present. After a long discussion, Norman decided to offer Peter an apprenticeship. This was agreed to by Peter's mother, Felicity, who had missed Norman for many years, and who realised that the financial incentives for apprenticing Peter could get her out of a financial hole she was in. The three agreed to a binding magical contract that required Norman to teach Peter and protect him for the term of the apprenticeship, Peter to follow the instructions of his mentor, and Felicity to hold onto Peter's earnings while he was away.

When leaving for his new home, Peter found a silver coin in the mud and gave it to Petunia so that she would not go hungry.

Felicity was skittish around magic, as her husband's Gareth's death had involved a magical force. This hesitation was exacerbated by Suzie, a gargoyle in the shape of a leopard, who, in conjunction with a money lender calling debts in, scared Felicity enough that she scoured a path to Norman's tower with wild magic.

Felicity was calmed, and together Norman and Peter set her up in new accommodation that would no longer require ongoing rent payments. In the process, Felicity gifted Peter with the tool set that his father had once owned.

Norman then took Peter to meet other mages in different

locales to teach him about magic. The first mage of this type was Scaramond, along with his apprentice Chance. Peter brought Petunia with him, despite being told not to, and Scaramond took a large amount of interest in her, offering powdered metals, volatile metals to increase its flame, and a bed made of silver and expensively furnished. This prompted Norman to warn Peter and Petunia about the hazards of accepting expensive gifts without knowing what the eventual cost would be.

While playing, Chance and Peter discovered that Peter was absorbing magical effects. After some testing, Scaramond and Norman determined that the reason Peter was having difficulty accessing his magical powers was that his magic reservoir was so large, it needed to fill before it could be accessed. The master mages agreed to annual visits to Scaramond's tower so that Peter could regularly access the vast library.

Peter gifted Scaramond with an ornate pin to assist with accessing his trigger. In return, Scaramond gave Peter a ceramic disc with a hole in the centre.

Upon returning to Norman's Tower, Peter spent the next two weeks constructing a water carrier to reduce the amount of labour he needed to undertake. At the end of construction, he discovered that the disc hid a portal to an ocean balcony, which enabled him to gather energy from the ocean.

A few days before Peter's 18th birthday, Norman was suddenly woken in the middle of the night by a summons to attend his mentor, Albert. Albert, Magus of Varthien, was on his deathbed and required Norman to assist in the process to call for a replacement Highmage to fill the spot he was about to vacate.

Peter woke to a sound he interpreted as an explosion – Norman's teleportation from the tower. Upon investigation, he found that Norman was no longer anywhere to be found. When Petunia woke to discover that her silver coin was no longer in her hoard, this startled her to the point where she accidentally set fire to the bush she called home. Peter became overwhelmed with emotion while he struggled to put out the fire and suddenly discovered how to move water when he doused the fire with magic.

Petunia became convinced that the only person who could have taken her coin was Reginald Cutler, the butcher's son, who, eight years prior, had killed all of her siblings thinking that they were earthworms. She told Peter that she knew who had stolen from her, and they set off to Pugton to face him.

In Pugton, the three ran into Felicity, whose growing distrust of magic became even more apparent because of a portal that had opened in her home. Once she had been calmed, Peter, Petunia, and Suzie moved on to Reginald's house, but hearing an argument happening at the front of the house, they went around to the cellar door. In the cellar, they discovered Petunia's mother bound to the floor and with mutilated wings. Out of necessity, Peter cut them from her body so they could release her from slavery.

When a battered Reginald discovered them freeing the gold dragon, Peter convinced him to flee his abusive family in Pugton.

Returning to Norman's tower, Misty confirmed that the coin had not been stolen by Reginald. Petunia gifted her hoard (sans the missing coin) to her starved mother to help give her nutrition. Suzie was sent to Bakar to fetch Scaramond, in the hope that he could assist a gravely wounded Misty.

Scaramond was not in Bakar. He was assisting Norman at Atinien Mountain to prepare for succession. Norman was startled to be chosen as the next Highmage by the succession box, and even more startled to then be named as Magus by Albert. He offered Albert Petunia's hoard coin as an item with imbued magic to keep him alive a bit longer, but Albert declined, stating that even if he had wanted to live longer, the coin wouldn't have enough power because it hadn't been given freely by its owner. Albert died a short time after.

Chance and Suzie teleported back to Norman's tower, having just heard the death dirge for the outgoing Magus.

Norman and Scaramond (who Norman discovered had been Albert's mentor and much older than his youthful face appeared to be) performed funerary rites for Albert, then returned with the succession box to Norman's tower a single day before Peter's 18th birthday. Norman asked Scaramond to return Petunia's coin to her, which he did.

Felicity arrived the next morning, and Norman discovered that she had failed to uphold her portion of the apprenticeship agreement, having spent a large portion of Peter's earnings to give herself better social standing. Norman, Peter and Felicity were unable to break out of the closed system of the binding, and so the magic started physically removing Peter's earnings from Felicity's body. Petunia was horrified to see the harm and gave the only item of her hoard that she had left – her coin. The magical process halted, then started reversing because of the added value to the system.

Scaramond and Chance, who had been out for a walk, arrived just in time to see the Felicity's recovery.

Scaramond made offers to Peter, Misty, Petunia, and finally to Felicity (who was now very scared of magic and unable to look at Norman in the same light), to join him in Bakar. They all accepted for various reasons. Peter discusses opening a mage school with Scaramond so they can stop using such a harmful method of binding apprentices.

Norman, who felt suddenly abandoned by everybody around him, declined to watch everybody leave. Only Suzie remained.

In the last chapter of book 1, we rewind by roughly 5000 years to the time of Argentus Barduce, at the end of the Interregnum War. Scaramond is running a school which has been identified as a place political unrest was spreading from. Argentus closes the school, and has had Scaramond set up the apprenticeship system and the Wizard Contracts that enforce it. It also hints that Scaramond may have been the creator of the succession box.

Introduction

1 OM Linter
Year of True Sight

Karastan Border

It had been raining for three days. Not a hard rain, not even a normal rain with actual drops that you could see, just a slight misty drizzle consistently laying a fine coat of moisture over everything. The kind of days you want to curl up inside with a good book and a soft, warm blanket.

Unfortunately, she was not inside. The world did not make things that easy for her. Instead, she had been trudging north, ever north. Her clothing lay heavy on her shoulders, dragging at her every step. The moisture sucked the warmth from her, increased the slight chafing from the incessant march, making the world just that bit more uncomfortable.

The roads around her were packed with people headed in the same direction, trying to do the same thing as her and escape the horrors that had come alongside the fighting. Each wore the same face. It was a blank face. A broken face. A face that had seen too many dreams die, that had seen loved ones die. That had seen buildings burn, friends turn on friends, entire worlds torn apart.

The mud that formed the road ahead of her was heavy like clay. It had been soaking in this rain, churned up by the feet of people moving like cattle. It was slippery to walk on but clung to the bottom of her once-blue skirt, slapping coldly against her shins with every step she took. As the bridge ahead came into view, a man who had been walking behind her for several days suddenly broke into a trot, jostling her. She slipped, falling headfirst into the mud. The man didn't look back. She had shared what little bread she had with him, but now she was as nothing to him.

He was stopped abruptly, she saw as she picked herself up from the ground, by official-looking men at the bridge. There was a little bit of murmuring that she could not quite catch at the start, followed by some louder posturing.

"Don't you know who I am?" floated over the air towards her. Personally, she hadn't heard of him until about three days ago; from what she gathered he was simply a farmer by the name of Rob. He had suffered from his crops being razed by the army that was supposed to be protecting his lands—denying the enemy resources, apparently. She held back, listening to the argument which now seemed to be heating up. The guards obviously did not know who he was. He was claiming to be an Earl, but he had no retinue, no paperwork, nothing to back up his inconsistent claim. A group of three guards circled him, one who was taking point with the questions, the other two moving behind the so-called Earl.

"You need the proper paperwork to be able to enter Karasta. You do not have the correct paperwork, or, it seems, any paperwork, therefore your entry is denied. Please step away from the bridge." The guard's voice was like a bullhorn, travelling loudly across the sea of people. With a light grumble, many of the people that were on the road moved to the side.

The farmer did not. He continued his argumentative posturing, holding firm to his claim to be someone of note, that he should somehow be above rules.

He did not see when one of the guards behind him drew a long sharp dagger and plunged it into his unprotected back. It struck him firmly on the left side, angled upwards to pass beneath the ribs, into the meaty flesh that cage of bone protected.

The farmer dropped. Surprisingly little blood came from the wound as the guard retrieved his dagger, then dragged the body to the side of the guardhouse. His voice rang out across the suddenly quiet masses. "Entry into the Kingdom of Karasta is closed to all who do not possess correct travel papers. Failure to comply with Karastan guards will lead to extreme measures, which may include imprisonment, flogging, or execution."

More people moved to the side of the road. She found herself alone in the middle of the road, with no other people between her and the bridge before her. Her grip tightened on the satchel she wore on her back. With a trembling breath she stepped forward, noting that people were already picking at the body of the farmer, removing anything of worth from his corpse.

The guard who had killed Rob looked down at her. He looked sweaty and uncomfortable in his armour, but that did not stop him from peering at her with the eyes of a bully. "Well, girly, come for a little taste of what happened to the guy before you?"

"I would like to pass the bridge please." She pulled out a long leather tube from her satchel, hands trembling involuntarily. Popping the fitted lid off, she fumbled to retrieve her papers. She cringed as she felt a soft tearing, the long, dangling seal catching on the seam of the tube.

She cringed again as the guard grabbed the paperwork from her. The heavy wax seal dangled, barely holding on by just a fraction of the paper that once held it. He squinted at the words, finding the pertinent name which had been written in large writing specifically for this purpose. "Clara Angmeyer. That you, girly?"

"Yes." Her voice sounded soft and hesitant, even to her own ears. She cleared her throat. "Yes," she said again, louder and more firmly.

"It says here that you should have people with you. Where is your maid? Where are your guards? Are you really this person?" He turned looking at his fellows and chuckled nastily. "I reckon we've got a thief here."

"My maid and my guards are dead," she said softly. "I hid while we were being attacked."

The guard leered at her. "You're not bad on the eyes, we might be able to come to… an arrangement."

The way he said it made Clara feel vile. She remembered the words of her governess— *You are of station. You are above the rabble. Never let them think otherwise.* Her spine stiffened.

Firmly she spoke now. "My papers are in order. You have seen them. You will now return them and allow me to pass. What is your name?"

The guard before her towered angrily, but he did not notice the two guards behind him step backwards.

"Perhaps we should…" the guard behind him uttered, looking at Clara respectfully.

"Perhaps you should just shut up when I'm talking to this peasant thief. I haven't had a right bollocking in two days." He slapped the papers into the chest of the other guard, never taking his eyes off Clara. "Now, little thief, how's about we take a few minutes in the guardhouse and get all of this sorted, eh?"

Clara's spine stiffened even further as she allowed her anger of the past few days to enter her voice. "I am not a peasant, nor am I a thief. Name. Rank. Regiment. I will see you disciplined."

As they had been talking, the guards behind had been looking carefully over Clara's documentation. One of them had run to the guardhouse while the other started tapping his fellow on the shoulder.

"Alf, Alf, you need to…"

The bullish Alf turned. "Will you shut the…"

He paled as he saw a fourth man emerge from the guardhouse, pulling his jacket into line.

"Miss Angmeyer," the new man said, with obsequious warmth in his voice, "Such a pleasure to assist the general's daughter in such trying times."

She turned to the new, obviously more superior, arrival. Her eyes flicked to the small pip on his lapel. "Captain. You will place this oaf under arrest immediately. He is not fit for the guard. He refused to allow me to pass, despite my paperwork being in proper order, accused me of being a thief, then insinuated that I might be able to pass anyway, even if my paperwork was suspect, if I lay with him. This suggests that he is easily bribable. I also witnessed him murder a man who was not a combatant, simply because the man was a pain in the ass. This is unbecoming."

Alf puffed out his chest, waving his arms dramatically. "Aw, cap, are you gonna listen to this little bint? She's what? Twelve? She knows nothing about what it's like here. Kick 'er to the curb. She's just raising trouble."

The captain looked at the two officers to the side. "Shackle him." He turned to the girl. "I trust that there will be no further issues at this station. We will make certain that this former guard makes no further problems for the Kingdom."

Inwardly, Clara heaved a sigh of relief. She had been wound like a spring under tension since leaving her mother's estate a week ago. The border crossing was an invisible line between confusion and stability. She harboured no illusions about seeing her father when she arrived at her new home — he was a very busy man after all — but here she would not be under the constant fear of becoming a pawn in someone else's game.

"Thank you, Captain. Could I trouble you for a cup of tea? It's been a harrowing few days."

The captain nodded. "Get Creevey and Artun to stand in while you pack away this lump of shite," he instructed the man who had taken Alf into custody. "I'll be taking care of this VIP for the next hour or so." He offered a short head nod to Clara. "If you come this way ma'am, I'll see to your comfort."

Chapter 1

Bakar

Misty followed the Scarred One as he walked her to an area behind the tower. The crushed gravel of the entry path earlier had spiked unpleasantly at the soles of her feet, unaccustomed to walking after so long chained to one spot, but now the fresh lawn soothed them, cool and springy.

She could see the dimensional pockets from the corners of her eyes, filling the vast gardens with their slanting distortions. The hidden structures bulged and pulsed, slipping against each other like magnets of the same polarity forced together.

"I know a story," she said to him gently as he led her towards one of the spacial distortions. "It's a sad story, but one my people have passed down, Mother to Daughter, for generations. The story is about a place called The Hidden Pathway. This place reminds me of that story."

The Scarred One tilted his head in the way dragons do when listening carefully. He slowed his walk. "I would be honoured to hear the wisdom of the Mothers."

"It is said that the First upon these soils each held a bond to a mage. They were bonds of love, not servitude, but they tied the life energy of the two bound. This is a gift to both, a dragon's food supply ensured through telepathic ties to one who can sense the metal below the soil, the mage's life lengthened, but death to one means pain and grief to the other for those ties mean shared sensation.

"The First scattered when they reached these soils, carrying their get across the lands. This story is of one of the First, the Mother who named herself *Orange Clouds in Twilight*, and her bound companion, your namesake, The Scarred One."

A flicker passed across the mage's face, but the tilt of his head remained.

"Together they reached a fertile land, with great beauty, a flowing river, and deep veins of metals that flowed in tangles beneath the ground. There, the Scarred One lay foundations for a great complex to raise the next generation, mages with wyrmlings in harmonious union. And there, Orange Clouds in Twilight dug into the earth and started her search for metals.

"Soon, a great hoard was amassed, for this was a rich place. Get and child alike found each other within the Scarred One's school, for he had not lain idle while his Mother dug deep. Both lay in the warmth of joy.

"And then the fall of the Mirror of Worlds. Humans and unbound mages alike had assailed it. Their intentions were unclear. But the Mirror shattered, and it broke the planet. One continent became five. Many died.

"Orange Clouds in Twilight was deep underground when the Mirror fell. She was buried; she was engulfed in magma. The Scarred One, however, was above. He remained safe.

"He was clothed in grief and pain for all his remaining days, and his soul became as scarred as his body. The places he had constructed for all were shrouded into folds, her pathway into the earth hidden, and he refused to instruct in bonding dragon to mage, for his pain was too great to place onto another.

"This was the story of *Orange Clouds in Twilight*, Greatest of Varthien's First and forever remembered."

Scaramond stopped before one of the distortions and flicked his hand. A hill appeared before them, a great cavern opened in its side, a long trek before darkness engulfed the downward-sloping tunnel.

"She still lives," he said, never looking at Misty as he stepped forward into the rocky hole. "It's the curse of my trigger. She burns, and I heal her. I can't stop—it's the bond. She is too deep for my fragile body to retrieve; she is bathed in magma that has melted her limbs and fused her teeth together, but she continues, trapped in the centre of the planet."

For an intense minute, the only sound was their tread on the stone. Then, Misty bowed her head.

"I shall add this knowledge into the story and pass it to every dragon who comes my way. I shall sing it in the skies so that all may hear. One of Varthien's First remains. The last of the First. This is sadness, but it is joy."

The Scarred One's eyes glistened with unshed tears. "Thank you for keeping her memory alive.

"The way forks here, and her first hoard chamber lies to the left. It is empty now, but you are welcome to build your hoard here. I will make it as comfortable as I can for you, and if there is anything I can supply, please ask.

"I would house you upstairs with your daughter, but my stairs were created for two legs, not four, and without wings you would be unable to reach the upper storeys."

The arch they passed through was so vast that for a moment Misty didn't realise it was a pinch point. As the Scarred One waved his hand to brighten the room with light, she saw that the arch was, indeed, a small entrance in comparison to the room it opened onto. Rugs were scattered over the flat stone floor, and cushions dotted the place, but other than that, it was, indeed, empty.

"My thanks, Scarred One. This looks to be an excellent place with room for hoard and room for growth." She bowed low to him. "I shall respect its bounds."

The mage placed two buttons onto the wall. "This first," he motioned, "will toggle the lights. The second will call me if you need anything. Anything at all."

INVITATION

Norman's Tower

Norman absently stroked Suzie's stone head as he looked through the correspondence that had started pouring in. Less than a week as Magus and already there were demands for his attention. Had he forgotten Albert getting this amount of mail or was it simply that people now remembered the Magus existed, he wondered?

A familiar crest stayed his hand from shuffling the envelopes, and he pulled it out from the mass of envelopes. A crest he had not seen in decades.

Sharpstone.

A shard of fear sliced at him, and he closed his eyes a moment. The base reaction was something he thought he had overcome years ago, but here it was again, the vague memory of cutting words making him feel like a child once more.

I am Magus, he thought. I am above this. She cannot hurt me.

With hesitant fingers, he cracked the wax seal and opened the envelope.

Magus Linter, it began. *Sharpstone Manor begs the honour of your attendance that you may be introduced to Karastan society…*

It went on for about a page, formal through and through, laying out the conditions of the event and who else would be invited to attend. There was nothing personal in the invitation, but his eyes lingered on the signature at the bottom.

Estrella Linter.

He had considered over the years that she may be dead, but her line had always been long-lived. Her mother, he recalled, lived into her nineties, having given birth to twelve children, Estrella being the youngest of the brood and married off to a noble fairly low in the pecking list but with enough fortune to curry favours and afford good living. She had a chance of living just as long, or longer.

Will she recognise me? The thought rang through his mind and he realised he had already decided to attend, despite knowing that it would be painful no matter the outcome.

Even so, his hand trembled as he penned his acceptance then placed it in the pile of outgoing correspondence.

EXPLORER

Bakar

The axe was warm in Peter's hand, smooth, the fine wood grain filling the pores of his skin like a thing alive.

The polished blade gleamed silver on the black that surrounded him, flashing in the sourceless light. His hands moved over the blade, feeling the sharp edge against his fingertips.

He felt his muscles tensing, lifting the axe, a sharp zing singing over his nerves. Horror filled him as he saw the beautiful golden dragon before him.

"No!" he cried as the axe came down. Peter felt like the axe was wielding him rather than the other way around as he struggled to change its path, but the golden wing fell away to a scream of pain that rang in his ears, echoing. A flood of liquid silver rained down over him, hot and slick, gliding over his skin, drowning him…

"Wake up, Peter," Petunia's small voice shouted into his ear as he flapped and flailed against the blankets. "It's a nightmare. You're dreaming…"

Slowly, Petunia's words broke through, her image superimposing itself upon the dream dragon, red flickering on the imagined gold.

"Ugh. Sorry," he mumbled groggily. "I didn't mean to wake you."

"It's okay. I was having a nightmare too," she said, snuggling into the crook of his neck.

He breathed deep, trying to shake off the memories that had formed the basis of the dream. *Misty's okay*, he reminded himself. *Her wings will grow back. They needed to be removed – they crippled her and kept her in slavery.*

He knew that his logic wasn't enough to salve the guilt he carried from that day, nor the sick feeling of having caused Petunia's mother pain. But he ran his fingers down the tiny dragon's spine in reassurance. "I'm fine. Are you alright? Something was on your mind yesterday and I know it was upsetting you, so you might as well tell me. What is it?"

"It's Misty," Petunia said. "She and I were talking, and her hoard is probably still out there. When she was caught, she was away from her den, so maybe nobody's found it yet. Maybe I could find it for her. We could go and get it and she'd be happy."

"Are you saying she's not happy now?"

"No, she's happy now because she's out of that basement, but she could keep being happy if her hoard is here."

Peter wound her tail gently between his fingers and considered her request. On one hand, he'd only just moved in and Scaramond might require his services. On the other hand, he thought he might be getting an idea of how his magic actually worked; it would be nice to test it out.

"Do we even know where Misty's hoard is," he asked.

"I do!" said Petunia, excited. "I showed her a map and she showed me where. It's in a jungle, near a swamp. I can show you in the morning. It will be fun!"

Happy, Petunia cuddled up under Peter's chin, and with the small comforting heat against his throat, he slept once more.

When the sun rose, Peter found a large, circular map in the

library, the size of a carpet. He lay it out on the floor and gazed intently at it. The map seemed to be old — some of the political borders had definitely shifted and there were country names he didn't recognise — but the landscape was likely unchanged. He hoped.

The small dragon didn't seem to mind the age of the map, pointing out a spot on the Eastern continent.

"It's there. Misty said she dug a hole in the side of a cliff in the jungle near a swamp. We should go."

Peter considered for a moment how frustrating it could be trudging through a jungle with a dragon whose mental age was that of a two-year-old human. But fondness won out, and he smiled.

"Let me just get some things together and we'll go."

Politeness bore obligations, which determined that Peter's first stop was Scaramond's apartment on the ninth floor. He had barely touched the door to knock when it swung open silently, revealing Scaramond's imposing desk which directly faced the entrance. Scaramond himself stood behind the desk, his back to Peter, looking out an implausibly located window which, by rights, should show the interior of the tower, but instead showed a vast yellow desert with a city in the distance.

"Petunia has asked me to help her find Misty's hoard. She's got a location, this side of the range, somewhere near the Lumbera River mouth. It's quite a ways, but I think I may be getting a handle on my abilities, so this would be a good test of transportation…"

"Good," Scaramond interrupted without turning around, "I was just thinking I needed some Pojeru fruit. At least ten but as many more as you can manage. They bruise easily and rot quickly once they've been removed from the vine, so you'll need to store them in stasis. The Lumbera River is perfect. Is a week sufficient? It will give me time to set up for your school idea."

"Yes, I think so." Peter smiled, happy that his new employer was so willing to mingle their objectives together.

The eighth floor was special. This was a magical test zone, a place to try out magical effects without preexisting magic to interfere with casting.

With his small pack firmly on his shoulder, he turned to Petunia.

"Hold on tight, I've never done this before, so I don't know what's going to happen."

Petunia grabbed hold of his upper arm and twisted her tail firmly around it. "You'll be okay," she reassured him.

He strode toward the centre of the room, intending to give himself as much space as he could in case he destroyed the building.

Suddenly, they were surrounded by lush ferns and trees, and his step forward was onto mud that rose unpleasantly around his shoe.

"Wow. That was awesome!" gushed Petunia. "Why do all you mages teleport so differently? Norman teleports like a clap of thunder and I feel sick afterwards, like he's rearranged all of my insides. When Scaramond teleports it's like I get tickles all over me. But this teleport was like you moved the whole world to where you are and I felt nothing. One second we were there, and the next minute we're here."

Peter looked around, trying to work out which direction they were facing. "I think it's because teleporting is hard. Everything is moving. We're moving on the planet, and the planet is moving around the sun, and the sun is moving around a space in the middle of a galaxy…"

"A dragon," interrupted Petunia.

"…What? Where?"

"In the middle of the galaxy. It's a dragon."

"O-oooh-kaaaay… a dragon. So, the sun is moving around a dragon, and the galaxy is moving around a space in the centre of the Universe…"

"That's a dragon too."

"Wait, what? I really don't understand."

"At the centre of the Universe, there lies the First," explained Petunia. "She's a Mother so great that she eats light itself. At the centre of each galaxy is another great Mother, and they all come to pay homage to her and feed her." She sighed wistfully. "Someday I will be bigger and I'll eat stars like the great Mothers."

"Interesting," said Peter, thinking that this may be the strangest thing that Petunia had ever said to him. "Well, as I was saying, there's a whole lot of things moving that need to be considered while teleporting, plus you've got to make sure you don't end up in the middle of a mountain or something…"

"I'd eat my way out," Petunia said matter-of-factly.

"Of course you would," Peter responded. "Me, on the other hand…"

"Oh, you're much too soft and squishy to eat your way out."

"That's right. Sort of. Any idea which way we're supposed to go?"

Chapter 4

CHIRREN

Qoth

Norman looked at the small, scribbled schedule in his hand. Everything was so intense right now, and he felt like he had barely a minute to himself. However, today's visit to Qoth would be a happy one, he thought, getting ready for the heat and sand. Happier, at least, than this evening's entertainment.

"Want to join me at the beach?" he asked Suzie.

He didn't expect a yes — she'd been doing so many things recently that she was looking a bit lean — and he was not wrong. She tilted her head in that way that said "No" and remained on her favourite beam in the rafters.

"Right then," he said with a chirpiness he didn't really feel, "I'll be off. Don't wait up for me — I'll be home quite late, I expect."

With that, he teleported.

The Qoth shoreline was one of the most beautiful places, Norman considered. Bright, white, powdery sand. Deep blue-green waters that lapped gently at the strand. Jewel green foliage. Cobalt sky so blue and unchanging that his eyes tried to superimpose spots and shapes in other colours over its perfection.

Barefoot, he walked to the water, dipping just his toe into the coolness. He could feel the sand shifting beneath his feet as the waves lapped the tiny grains away, replacing them with other grains over the top of his foot.

Beyond the reach of his vision, he knew, was a long island that broke the wild surf, enabling these calms. This was the perfect breeding ground for the Chirren—the waters warm and the birthing pools protected. He closed his eyes, feeling the wind against his face, fresh and fragrant with the salt tang.

When he heard clicking behind him, he turned, his arms outstretched. There, on the beach behind him, stood a chirren, standing on its four walking legs, its four manipulator legs outstretched, it's two chelipeds relaxed before it, claws clasped before its gills.

Norman breathed deeply, remembering the feel of hot spice on his tongue that allowed him to understand and be understood, no matter the language.

"Magus," the chirren said, "I welcome you to Wamanil clan. Be family." It relaxed its manipulator legs and motioned for him to step forward.

Norman put his arms down. "I am delighted to be family with Wamanil. Let us meet."

Together they strode along the shore. Unaccustomed to walking on sand, Norman felt like his calves were being stabbed by hot pokers by the time they reached the sheltered river inlet that the clan currently called home.

The clan was a large one, known along this coast as the preeminent clan that was the centre for trade with land-dwellers. Their small huts were simple, made of unworked branches and woven grasses, but elegantly assembled, each as unique as the next.

Evidence of their trade with nearby human settlements abounded, many chirren wearing woven necklaces that bore bright glass beads, and he saw children playing together on Mardane sets or playing a version of Jacks that involved balancing the jack on a clawed cheliped while flipping multiple balls with the manipulator legs on the same side.

The chirren who had initially met with Norman introduced himself as Chk, and as they wove through the maze of huts Chk introduced him to every chirren they met. Norman struggled to find differences between each chirren, and after the first dozen introductions he realised that he would not be able to remember names anyway. The clan was more than a hundred strong, and if he was being introduced to everyone, the likelihood of remembering more than two or three individuals was low.

Wherever he went, the children gathered around, attentive to the strange figure in their midst. Some brought him small gifts—flowers, polished shells, smooth stones, and when a chirren gave him a basket of grass and bark offset with green and blue wool, he was grateful to be able to empty his hands of the trinkets he'd been given. In return, he knelt before it and pulled a cord out of his pocket that was stranded with green beads.

"Thank you for such a fine and thoughtful gift. I needed a basket. Please accept this necklace. The cord will never rot or break, and the beads will always catch the light."

The young chirren clicked its chelipeds together in delight as it fastened the cord around its head then ran off to show the treasure to friends and parents.

"You have found a friend there," said Chk. "Her name is Em. She will be reaching her adulthood soon. She is one of our most talented weavers and we expect great things of her."

After an uncountable number more introductions, Norman was led to a large space in the middle of the settlement. It was notable for its access to the river mouth, the banks having been shaped to form small pools, some bearing eggs and very young chirren, others being used as storage for mussels, clams, crabs and fish.

He was given a shaded seat that seemed especially designed for human visitors, and so, finally able to rest his legs,

Norman sat. From his vantage facing the riverbank, he watched chirren dive into the deep channel, coming up bearing seaweed or jellies to bring ashore and dump onto large tables set into the ground for permanent use.

The midday meal appeared an informal affair, chirren standing around in small groups, eating from the tables provided. Norman was given a large wooden platter, obviously an item purchased through trade with humans, which Em swiftly grabbed from him and ran off to fill with delicacies. She brought it back loaded with the freshest, most succulent morsels — a little of everything so that he could taste and try things he had never tried before.

He considered her kindness and decided that at some point in the future he would return, bringing delicacies from all across Varthien to pay in kind, so that she and all her clan could try things they had never been able to try before.

The chirren provided a stuffed and tired Norman with a hammock and he napped, the tropical sunshine drawing away all the stress and urgency that he had felt these past days. Then, in the afternoon, the sun dropping bit by bit to meet the horizon, he entertained the children with green and blue light shows, telling stories with the shapes he formed against the side of a hut.

As darkness fell and he was required elsewhere, he felt a twinge of sadness that he had not seen Em to speak to her since his exquisite meal.

Chapter 5

Sharpstone Manor

Norman teleported directly to the entrance foyer of Sharpstone Manor, still barefoot and covered in sand. He recalled the first time he had seen Albert in this very same room, barefoot and trailing mud along the polished marble with his long robes, and considered the mirroring of his mentor's appearance to be fitting for his reappearance at Sharpstone. With a frisson of glee, he hoped that the sand he traipsed in would irreparably scratch the marble surface.

A butler hurried up to him. "Sir was not expected to simply… appear, sir. Sir was expected at the…"

"Magus. I'm not a Sir. I'm the Magus."

The butler bowed low. "My deepest apologies, Magus. May I show you to the ballroom where most other guests are already…"

"I do know my way, thank you. I used to live here, you know."

"Of course, but Milady…"

"Oh. Yes. She'll take it out on you, won't she." The look on the butler's face affirmed Norman's assumption. "Better announce me then. Full title — Highmage Magus Norman Linter, Earl of Sharpstone Manor."

"But…"

"She may object, but she's not the actual boss here. I am. I will make certain that there is no fallback onto you."

"Very well, sir… Magus."

The butler walked before him, opening the large double doors and yelling while trying to conceal the look of glee on his face: "Announcing His Arcane Majesty, Highmage Magus Norman Linter, Earl of Sharpstone Manor."

Norman stepped forward, winking slyly at the butler. "Nice touch," he whispered, as he swept into the room.

Estrella Linter rushed over, pale-faced. "What? Earl of what? And what are you wearing? What is that horrendous thing on your face?"

Norman raised a self-conscious hand to his beard, then straightened. "Father is dead, my elder brother died without children. I kept track, you know. That makes me Earl by right of birth. Now show me around, *Estrella*." He put emphasis on the name, making certain she noted that he didn't acknowledge her as mother.

Estrella swallowed heavily, perhaps realising that her seat in this place was by no means assured, then stiffened her spine.

"This way."

Estrella wove amongst the guests, who all stopped to stare at the barefoot man in plain linen robes who was dropping sand wherever he went. A ripple of motion followed wherever she went, as people all bowed as Norman passed, respecting his new station. She stopped before a dark-haired man, clad in a richly embroidered red silk coat and coal-black pants. His fingers bore golden rings that were mostly hidden by the draping lace of his cuffs.

"Your Majesty, may I present my daughter, Norma Linter. Norma, this is his Royal Majesty, Hrodolf, King of Karasta."

Hrodolf cocked an eyebrow at Norman's appearance, so

Norman introduced himself more thoroughly.

"Norman Linter, Highmage Magus, Earl of Sharpstone. It's an honour, Majesty." He started to bow, but Hrodolf stopped him with a hand, then bowed deeply himself.

"You outrank me, your Arcane Majesty. Under the proper protocols I bow to you. However, we do need to take some time for your investiture, as I understand you've been out of country for some time." The king turned to his steward who waited patiently behind him and muttered briefly in his ear.

"Is now a suitable time, Magus?"

Norman smiled. "Of course, Majesty."

At a nod, the steward stepped forward and called loudly, "Hear ye, hear ye, attend his Majesty, all. The court of Hrodolf, King of Karasta, is called to session."

The murmur of conversation stopped abruptly and everyone in the ballroom turned to face Norman and Hrodolf. Estrella's eyes were wide and her breath fast, Norman noted, as if nothing was happening the way she intended.

"Attend, all, to the investiture ceremony of Norman Linter, Earl of Sharpstone by right of birth. Do you, Norman Linter, swear fealty to Hrodolf, King of Karasta, to act in faith to him, obey his lawful commands, and to never cause harm to him or his people and office? Do you swear to act in his favour with all persons in good faith and without deceit? Do you swear to come to his aid in times of distress, bearing such arms as is appropriate?"

"I do so swear."

Hrodolf lay a light hand on Norman's shoulder. "Rise, Earl of Sharpstone."

A light smattering of applause followed.

"The court of Hrodolf, King of Karasta is brought to a close," called the steward. The conversation started to rise again, but then ceased abruptly as the steward called again, "Hear ye, attend all. The court of his Arcane Majesty, Highmage Magus Norman Linter, is called to session."

Norman was caught by surprise, but not more surprised than his mother, who was breathing so fast and had gone so pale that he thought she might pass out.

"Attend, all, to the ceremony of fealty. Do you, Hrodolf, King of Karasta, swear fealty to his Arcane Majesty, Norman Linter, Highmage Magus of Varthien, to act in faith to him, obey his lawful commands, and to never cause harm to him or his people and office? Do you swear to act in his favour with all persons in good faith and without deceit? Do you swear to come to his aid in times of distress, bearing such arms as is appropriate?"

"I do so swear."

Norman lay a light hand on Hrodolf's shoulder. "Rise, King Hrodolf of Karasta."

The steward spoke again. "Any who wish to swear fealty to the office of the Arcane Majesty, please step forward and be recognised."

A great swell of nobles pushed forward, pushing Estrella further from the front, away from Norman and Hrodolf, and for the next twenty minutes he was occupied with nobles determined to swear fealty to his station. Then, in the time until the dinner bell sounded, he was passed from one noble to the next in a dizzying array of introductions and obsequiousness as people vied for his attention.

The dining hall was elaborately arrayed, glittering metal carafes shining on every table, with bowls of fruit and platters of cheese and bread scattered for nibbling on between courses. A small placard sat at each plate, naming the intended recipient. Towards the end of the hall a platform had been erected with the high table atop it, and all other tables were perpendicular to this one so that no matter where in the room someone sat, they could turn to face the high table.

Norman was escorted forward by an usher, directly to the high table.

"Your place has been prepared, your Arcane Majesty. I hope you enjoy your meal."

Norman was about to sit down, but Hrodolf lay a hand on his shoulder.

"You're fresh into this," he muttered, "But this table setting is all wrong. I shouldn't be in the centre seat like this—that's yours. Will you accept my sword as your protection this evening?"

"Of course," Norman said, not quite understanding the issue.

"How long did you say you've been out of country?"

"I left when I was eight and I haven't been back since, so… 36 years?"

The king clicked his fingers and his steward stepped forward. "Colton, given the events earlier, would you say this is accidental or deliberate?"

The steward puffed his lips out, thinking. "It could be deliberate. Could be ignorance of protocol. Could be underestimating the power of the Magus."

"Let's not take any chances, eh?" Hrodolf said. "All of my plates, glasses, and cutlery, physically one place to the left. Have one of mine move it all. That way, any poisons meant for me will continue to be mine. And have them rearrange the seating for the rest of the table. It won't do to have someone seated in the wrong spot. Meanwhile, I want you—mind you, YOU, not someone else and definitely not one of the Dowager Countess' staff—to take all of the crockery and cutlery from this seat determined to be for the Magus, and replace it all with freshly cleaned crockery and cutlery. Better change the linens as well while you're at it.

"We'll see you sorted," Hrodolf said to Norman. "Might be worthwhile for you to get yourself someone like Colton here. He acts as my servant, protocol guide, bodyguard… There are too many things to think about when you're in a high position."

As movement increased at the high table, shuffling seat positions and altering plating arrangements, Estrella hurried up.

"Is everything alright," she asked, looking flustered. "What's happening?" Belatedly she remembered to curtsey to her king.

"Nothing to worry about, Estrella," said Hrodolf smoothly. "There were some mix-ups with the seating arrangements—probably one of your servants getting it wrong."

"But I double checked everything myself!" Estrella complained, not realising that Hrodolf was handing her an easy out.

"Nevertheless," he said, raising an eyebrow. "My steward is currently overseeing mitigation for potential assassination attempts against the Magus. It would be a terrible thing if there were anything… untoward… to happen tonight."

Estrella's mouth opened and closed repeatedly, like a fish stranded on a beach. Then she curtseyed awkwardly once more. "Of course, your Majesty. I will make certain that everything is correct from hereon in."

Once Norman's new dinner setting had been placed and all the place names had been righted, Norman looked around.

"Why is everyone still standing," he whispered to Hrodolf.

"Because you are," Hrodolf whispered back. "You hold the highest status in this room, so you sit, then I sit, then everyone else sits."

"Oh." Norman felt somewhat foolish and pulled his seat back, only to have it taken from him by a servant.

"People expect you to never use your hands for anything," Hrodolf whispered. "Let staff do things for you. It makes people happier, I've found."

So, Norman allowed a servant to seat him, and another to lay a napkin across his lap, and a third to fill his glass. Then a fourth brought out a steaming crockpot of broth on a wheeled cart and filled the bowls for each of the people on the high table, Norman first. A delicate and unfamiliar scent wafted from the creamy broth, white lumps floating in a pinkish fluid, topped with a sprinkling of fresh chives.

"What is this course," Hrodolf asked.

"Chirren, Majesty, in a lightly spiced potage."

Norman looked at the broth before him, thinking of his day with the Wamanil clan.

"Chirren. As in, actual chirren? The size of a man, lots of legs, that chirren?"

"Yes, Majesty." The server bowed and moved on to the next bowl.

Hrodolf saw the look of distress on Norman's face. "Is something wrong?"

Norman felt his gut roll. "Yes. Something is definitely wrong." He stood. "Estrella Linter, what is the meaning of this?"

Estrella rose from her seat and hurried over, a cross look on her face. "Do call me Mother, Norma, you're making a scene again."

"A scene? I'm making a scene? You served me chirren!"

"Yes. Don't worry, it's very fresh. It fouled the nets this afternoon, just off the Qoth border. I'd already organised to take whatever the haulage was on that boat for this feast, so when they said I could have an entire chirren, I was ecstatic! It's not often you get a catch like this."

"Do you know where I was today? I was being welcomed into a chirren clan as family. You've just served me one of my subjects! Not just one of my subjects, one of my relatives! Is it not enough that you sell me when I was a child, now you're eating people?"

"Oh, hardly people, Norma…"

"Stop calling me Norma," he roared. "My name is Norman, and you will address me appropriately to my station." He felt a strange thrill course through him, the scent of the chirren broth in his nose, and bands of magical force drove Estrella to the floor, spreadeagled before him. "You are not my mother. You gave up that right when you sold me to Albert Tarandeer. You are an old woman who has just lost every ounce of status that she was squeezing from my father's corpse, because you are no longer welcome in my manor."

"She sold you?" Hrodolf looked at the prone woman in disgust.

"Under the guise of a mage contract, but I recall her words. It wasn't a negotiation. It was a sale." Norman dropped his napkin onto the table and strode to the kitchen, servants hurrying before him to open doors and clear the path. And there, lying on a kitchen bench, was a chirren, quartered and gutted, with its exoskeleton cracked in several places that quartering wouldn't reveal. It was smaller than most of the adults Norman had met, and with a flipping feeling in his gut he realised that this was still a child.

Then his eyes fell upon a glint of colour, a strand of green beads caught around a severed cheliped. Tenderly, he gathered up the remaining parts of the chirren corpse into his arms and carried them back to the dining hall.

"This is a person." His voice rang out to all of the people in the hall, which seconds before had been abuzz with voices speculating on this exciting turn of events. "She is a child. I met her this morning. She gave me a basket that she wove herself. I gifted her the strand of beads caught around her claw.

"Her name was Em."

POLITICS

Sharpstone Manor

Hrodolf looked at the distressed mage standing in the middle of the ballroom, carrying the remains of the lobster-like chirren. He puckered his lower lip between thumb and forefinger, considering the ramifications, then motioned to Colton.

"What do you make of this," he asked as quietly as he could.

"Sss," Colton said the familiar tone he made whenever he was considering something difficult. "It's an oversized lobster and he's upset? It's not a good look."

"I agree, but he's an unknown quantity right now. Best to keep him on side—I have a feeling that little display with the Dowager Countess may be the thin edge of the wedge, and I'd rather not be on the receiving end of that temper. Send someone at speed to the palace, get a room turned down for the Magus, and have them get rid of all chirren from the kitchens. I don't care what they do with it, so long as it's not there when we arrive. Have someone from the stables prepare a catafalque for this body. I'll pre-empt him with a decree in the morning denouncing all consumption of chirren. Bloody mages—unpredictable. At least I knew how far I could push old Albert."

"I'll see to it at once." Colton disappeared through a curtain to the side. Hrodolf knew everything would get done promptly.

He stood and approached Norman, head bowed, and put a hand on his shoulder. Then he turned to face the nobles assembled.

"This is a travesty," he said sternly, allowing his projection training to amplify his voice. "I never believed it necessary to tell my people not to kill and eat other intelligent peoples. But here we are, and this is the result. I beg that Our Mage Linter will stay within the palace tonight, that tomorrow we may return Em to her people with the respect due to this dire turn of events. I shall be issuing a decree in the morning making it illegal to consume the flesh of chirren, or to kill chirren. I invite you all to attend the funeral procession in the morning. Wear appropriate shoes for a long cortege."

A servant hurried forward with a pristine, white sheet and laid it at the feet of the Magus.

"Lay down your burden, Magus, that we might carry it for you," Hrodolf intoned with as much gravity and pathos that he could summon.

Norman sighed deeply, his red eyes closing briefly, then he knelt and gently laid Em's remains onto the sheet, rearranging the pieces until they fit closely together. He placed a hand briefly on the head of the dead chirren, ran his fingers over the beads wrapped around the claw, then picked up one side of the sheet and folded it across her body. Hrodolf knelt opposite the Magus and folded over the other side of the sheet. Together, they swaddled Em's body for transport as neatly as they could. Then, standing, they found themselves surrounded by nobles jockeying to be pallbearers.

Hrodolf didn't really care who helped lift the body. He wasn't going to be looking at them anyway. He simply noted that they managed to sort themselves out quietly as he took his place at the head of the wrapped chirren, hoping that there wasn't too much seepage as they made their way to the front door. It wouldn't do to have people slipping over on those polished marble floors in the foyer.

Step by step they moved down the stairs, and Hrodolf breathed a sigh of relief as he saw that Colton had organised that his carriage be prepared, and a suitable wagon draped for the corpse. Feeling a pang of hunger, he hoped that Colton had organised some snacks for the trip home. He considered that it would be impolitic to suggest that dinner at the manor be continued, as the kitchen was now suspect. A bit of cheese might be nice, some dried fruit, maybe some nuts.

They lay the wrapped body onto the wagon, carefully, so as not to shuffle the pieces too badly. It was, thought Hrodolf, somewhat like a sack of potatoes, shifting and sagging whenever someone moved at slightly the wrong time. Once she was in place, he thankfully stepped away from the body, turning to look for a place to wash up.

Someone had anticipated this need, as a burly servant stood carrying a deep basin filled with clean water. Hrodolf motioned for Norman to go first, who dipped hands deep into the basin and cleaned off the blue fluids that covered his arms, then Hrodolf followed, glad to rid himself of the sticky feeling. It did nothing for the smell, and Hrodolf resigned himself to smelling like a fishmonger for the four-hour journey to his capital, Lanrash. A bath would be nice, he thought as he patted down his arms with the soft towel provided, and clean clothes that smelt like lavender.

"After you, Magus," Hrodolf said, motioning Norman to the enclosed carriage. "The journey to Lanrash is fairly easy-going but takes some time. I had originally planned on staying at the manor tonight, but circumstances being what they are, that's no longer the preferable option. I'll have some men stationed to make certain your wishes are met, and that the Dowager Countess leaves immediately upon collecting her personal effects. Have you allowed her to get off the floor yet?"

A look of horror briefly flashed over Norman's face. "Oops. I'd forgotten about her. Better let her up." His shoulders untensed as he climbed up the carriage steps and into the carriage. "Nice upholstery."

Hrodolf smiled. "Yes. I like this carriage. Comfortable seats. And if you lift the arm rest there, you should find some refreshments."

Norman lifted the armrest as Hrodolf settled into a seat. "It's going to be dark in here, but I can get one of the servants to light us a..." his voice trailed off as a soft light filled the small space. "Oh. Never mind then. Handy to have a mage. I don't have one in court right now. Perhaps you could recommend one sometime." Hrodolf peered into the armrest. Cheeses, dates, apricots, apples, and a carafe of unknown liquid — probably a fruit juice, knowing Colton. He considered it for a moment as the carriage started moving, then decided against the chance of spilling more fluids onto his already soiled clothing.

"So, tell me about yourself..."

Chapter 7

Karastan Border

Clara shivered, feeling the damp seeping through again. It had been nice in the guard station—they'd had a fireplace going with a stew pot bubbling, and the Captain had allowed her a bowl and a chance to dry some of her clothes while he'd organised an escort for her. There had been a lot of raised voices, some sharp sounds like someone was getting whipped, but she had been content to ignore it all to get the stew into her belly and warm the clothing on her back.

The rickety stool she sat on wasn't comfortable, but she'd been nodding off by the time the Captain returned.

"You're in luck," he had said in a loud voice, startling her into alertness. "We're shorthanded as is, and now we're down another man, but we've got a supply vehicle that needs to return to Lanrash. It's not a fancy carriage like you'll be accustomed to, but it's dry, mostly."

Indeed, it *was* mostly dry, if a little uncomfortable. The wagon was covered with an oiled canvas, the floor was strewn with hay, and boxes of seemingly random supplies vied with her for space. But without a fire to warm her anymore, the chill of her still damp clothing sapped the heat from her bones.

She wished she had packed some heavier clothing, but it had been so hot when she left home, and she hadn't anticipated the journey to take this long, nor so much of it to be on foot. She longed for the clouds to break, just for a little while. Sweltering, sweaty heat would be preferable to this long, drawn out, week-long drizzle.

She eyed the shackled Alf at the other end of the wagon. He seemed to be chatting in a low voice through the raised flap of oiled canvas to the driver, who was quite chummy with the prisoner. The words were mostly concealed by the sound of the wheels on the gravel road, but sprinkles of laughter occasionally floated back on the air to her. She couldn't see the relief driver, who sat opposite Alf but was hidden from view by a high stack of boxes, but she thought that some of the laughter was also his.

She hugged herself, as much to self-soothe her misery as to warm herself. Somehow, she had felt safer alone, on foot, than she did in this swaying carriage, protected by military men. Pulling some of the hay into a pile, she settled herself down into a small huddle and allowed herself to sleep.

Clara felt like she had only dozed, but woke abruptly when rough hands gripped her around her upper torso and another set of hands grabbed her legs.

"Watch she doesn't kick you in the face," a rough voice said from behind. "That's how I lost a tooth that time, remember?"

A mean laugh came from the man gripping her legs as she bucked. "That's what comes of trying to suck her toes. I have no intention of putting my face anywhere near this one. She's a goldmine, but only if we play it right." He puffed as she continued to struggle, trying to release her arms, her legs, throwing her head back to try to connect with the person behind her. "What're you doing, Alf? Help us, blast you!"

Alf came into view, chewing on a stem of grass. "Thought you guys said she'd be easy," he chuckled, swinging the shackles that had previously been around his wrists. "Give us a wrist then. Hold her steady. Once she's got irons on, it'll be easier to control the little bint."

Clara tried to twist away, but within moments the iron had snicked its way around her wrists, biting hard against the bone. Panting hard, she glared at her captors.

"You'll all hang when my father gets hold of you," she spat at the men, being as loud and brave as she could.

"Or we'll get a good payday and live large in Jerros, eh boys?" the driver said with a raised lip that was as much a sneer as a smile, never taking his eyes off Clara. "They got these fruit things, spiky on top, but like the sweetest honey. My cousin told me. And the nut-brown girls who like the foreign sounding guys…"

Alf bumped the driver with a shoulder. "You wouldn't know what to do with a girl if you got one, Russ. Come on, Fig, do you have that stuff for writing yet?"

Clara hadn't noticed that the hands had disappeared from behind her, but she looked around at where they had been and saw that the relief driver was fumbling with a sack. She noted that they were in a ramshackle yard, vines overgrowing a house that was half-collapsed, an old shed with a tree growing through its roof, the remains of wooden fencing.

"Like what you see, milady?" Alf asked sarcastically. "Your estate awaits." He prodded her forward. The grass in the small clearing was hip-high, but a barely noticeable path seemed to have been pushed into the grass by someone recently, flattening some of the tall stems. She moved along the path of least resistance, noting everything as she strode towards the lichen-covered stucco walls. The door had long fallen away, leaving a yawning black mouth leading into what remained of the house.

She recalled her father's words. If you are ever taken, pay attention. Note everything around you. Look for your captor's weaknesses. Be compliant. Make him think you are small and weak. Be his friend. Make him want to protect you. But don't forget you are a prisoner, and when you see good opportunities, work to free yourself.

So, though she wanted to shrink away from the darkness

where anything could await her, she complied with the steady pressure on her back and stepped into the unlit room ahead of her.

The interior of the house was not as dark as she had first feared. Not only was the roof caved in at one end of the building, its big beams resting in the dirt and covered in a curtain of vines, other holes in the roof allowed the light to filter softly through green leaves. The floor was covered with a spongy layer of rich, decomposed mulch that smelled pleasantly earthy.

The sharp pressure in her back motioned her towards the far end of the room, away from the collapsed area and towards a more stable looking area that included a fireplace. The room was devoid of windows, but included small vents along the eaves, some of them blocked up with small birds' nests. Something in a dark corner scuttled away at the sound of people, and Clara hoped she wouldn't be sharing a space with strange creatures that might try to cuddle up to her in her sleep.

Clara eyed the chimney. With any hope, it had long been blocked with debris. "I'm still very cold," she said in the most pleading voice she could muster, "Would it be alright if we had a fire to warm up?"

Alf grunted. "Eh, Russ, the princess wants a fire. Any wood out there?" he yelled.

Surreptitiously scuffing her foot on the floor, Clara noted that flagstones lay beneath the soil. "If there's a broom, I could make it nicer in here. I'm scared of spiders." Clara worked to put a little tremor in her voice. In truth, she liked spiders, but she knew that many people were afraid of them, sometimes including people that seemed otherwise tough.

"And bring a broom if you can find one!" he yelled, louder, looking suspiciously at the corners AND confirming Clara's suspicions.

Shortly after, Russ entered the room dragging an old, dry log and carrying a hoe.

"No brooms. But this should clear up some of the muck off the floor." He peered around. "I've stayed in worse places, I suppose. This could be right cheery with light."

Clara held out a shackled hand for the hoe, and Russ looked at her suspiciously. "Don't feel right giving a weapon to a prisoner."

"She's a kid. What's she gonna do," asked Alf, "Kill us with a garden tool then magic those shackles off? Fig's got the key, and he's on his way to the capital. Let her do the housework things. That sort of stuff makes chicks happy."

Clara grabbed the hoe, glaring intently at Russ. "I just want a space where I'm not going to have creepy crawlies all over me," she lied. Then, deliberately choosing to act clumsier than she really was, she turned and started scraping away at the dirt in the corner, pulling it away from the wall.

The captors lay a small fire, which made the room hot and smoky. As Clara had foreseen, something was blocking the chimney. She bent low over her task, trying to take in the fresher air towards the ground and blinking away the irritants from the smoke.

Alf seemed to hold a lot of sway over Russ, and his casual treatment of her played directly into her hands. A few minutes into her methodical clearing of the dirt, he became bored of watching her, and his coughing showed that he was having difficulties in the smoky air.

"How about we see what else is in those crates? Bet there's all sorts of good haul we've picked up." Without looking at her or his companion, he headed for the door. Russ followed quickly, glad to be out of the smoke.

Clara acted quickly, dropping to her knees and scrabbling in the dirt for a slight glint she had spotted in the firelight. A thin butter knife found her fingers, and she gasped in delight. Perfect! With bated breath, she slid the blade up the latch of the manacle, just like she and her father had practiced time and again, trying to shim the internal workings away from the teeth on the cuff.

Suddenly, the pressure around her wrist eased, and her hand was free. She tucked the bread knife into the waist of her clothing and grabbed the hoe, sneaking across to the collapsed area of the roof.

She could hear Russ and Alf talking outside. Their voices were muffled, as if they were on the other side of the wagon. Carefully, as quietly as she could, she spread her weight across the old roof beams, testing their integrity. They felt solid, if a little crumbly and didn't give when she pushed against them. Satisfied that they could bear her weight, she pushed the hoe through the leaves that blocked the light, finding a spot to balance her makeshift weapon, then with careful hands and feet, she scaled the beams.

Ducking low so she wouldn't be visible, she drew up the hoe, then, wincing at the sound, she moved the parted leaves back into place. She gazed into the jungle around the small yard. Small trees had capitalised on the available light and had thrust their thickest masses of leaves into the sun so that the way looked almost impenetrable. It would be easy to get lost in the mass of green that rose up around the tiny house, but equally, it would be harder for her captors to locate her. Quietly, she crept down the side of the house and into the trees

Chapter 8

Karastan Jungle

Clara had run far from the ruined house before she stopped to consider that perhaps that was a mistake. The jungle was dark, but she assumed it was still daytime because there was enough light to see by. There was no way to tell which direction she was travelling in, and she didn't have a clue where she was, so there was no way of knowing which direction she should be headed in.

Breathing deeply, she forced herself to become calm. There was no sound of anyone seeking her out, so now was a good moment to stop and take stock of her situation. She slid her back down a wide tree to sit at its base, where she cleared a small area of dirt.

There was the hoe. It was good, sturdy construction, with a well-worn wooden shaft and a sharp metal edge. It would be a clumsy weapon, but she thought she could defend herself with it if she needed to.

The butter knife was still tucked in her waistband. Pulling it out, she noted that its edge was blunt, but the thin metal was flexible and now bent a little from using it as a shim earlier. Using her off-hand, she worked the blade into the shackle still attached to the wrist on her dominant hand, shimming the teeth away from the latch until it swung open and dropped to the ground.

She lay the butter knife down and arrayed the shackle next to it.

Digging her hand into the folds of her skirt, she found the opening at her hip and reached inside to tug on the pocket. Thankfully, it hadn't been taken by the three deserters. They either hadn't noticed it, or thought it didn't have anything in it. In truth, it was mostly empty, but deep in the corner she found a small flint.

She could have shouted in joy, if her mind was not so focussed on the precarious situation she was in. She settled for a wide smile. Flint and metal were a good start to survival, and there was enough iron amongst her small hoard that she could fetch a good price at a blacksmith or a merchant. She stuffed the shackles into the pocket, which, it turned out, was only just wide enough to fit their bulky shape. The flint was dropped in there as well, and Clara hoped it wouldn't rattle too much as she walked. She stuffed the butter knife back into her waistband and tried to remember what her father had told her about orienteering.

People build settlements near water, she thought. Water flows downhill. But bigger watercourses will be more difficult terrain because the jungle gets hungry for the light. It's easier to walk when you're on the tops of the hills because the trees keep the light out.

I need to find a road. Roads lead to places where there are people. I need to see the sun. It will tell me which way to travel. I don't want to go South — South is Qoth and the border. Lanrash is West, beside the sea. I want to go West.

Clara looked up for any hint of the sun, but all she saw was occasional dapples of white far above — not enough to tell her which direction the light was coming from. She sighed, thinking she shouldn't have moved so far away from the ruin — that she might not be able to find it again. It must have had a road leading to it, and if she'd circled the area quietly, the men might never have thought to look for her in that direction. But it would have been noisy and hard to walk because there was so much undergrowth.

Clara's stomach growled, but she ignored the pangs. It

wasn't the first time she'd been hungry in the past few weeks, and she knew she could survive it, especially because she had the stew earlier. She wondered how long ago that had been. She had no idea how long she had slept in the wagon. Of greater importance was thirst, she remembered her father saying. Thirst would kill a person in just days, whereas hunger took a longer route. She circled back in her mind. Water flows downhill.

With her mind made up, she stood and gauged the slope of the land. Then, with a direction decided, she walked downhill.

Sometimes downhill isn't a very useful direction, Clara thought an immeasurable time later. The land undulated, and occasionally she found herself in marshy bogs where the land dipped with nowhere to go but uphill again. These places smelled, and tiny biting insects crawled over her skin, searching for the blood that pulsed behind that thin barrier. She refused to drink the water from the ground in these places, preferring to seek out the wide-leaved succulents that gathered dew next to their heart like tiny cups. The water there smelled fresh and sweet, not like the noxious tones of rot that the ground water conveyed. The light was fading quickly, and Clara, not wanting to spend her night in such a dark, dank place, lifted her heavy feet to walk uphill once more, leaning heavily on the hoe as if it were a walking stick.

By the time Clara felt flat ground beneath her again the light was gone. With a deep sigh, she sat in a spot between the trees, with a large fern behind her to block the sneaky breeze. She pulled together twigs and leaves from the area around her, as dry as she could find, and gathered them in an area she had cleared with her hoe, using it like a rake. Her fingers trembled as she pulled out first the shackles then the flint, and struck the flint against the iron, holding them low near her gathered tinder.

Clara hated lighting fires. She never managed to get the sparks in the right place. It always took her ages to get things to light. Even if she got things smouldering, there was no guarantee of a flame… Her litany of self-flagellation continued in her tired mind, and when a small fire started she stared at it in disbelief at first, before realising that she needed to feed it something larger if she wanted to keep it burning. She looked around for some larger branches.

The burgeoning flame was forgotten instantly, however, when she saw a tiny glow moving toward her. The spot of light wove through the trees, a sound of voices travelling on the wind, just faint enough that Clara could not distinguish words.

Closer it came, not a person, but a flying shape with an inner glow, wings like a dragonfly. Closer, and she saw it was the shape of a tiny person, a woman the size of Clara's hand, pale skin, with a flowing silken dress cinched at the neck and the waist, hiding her legs and feet, her outstretched arms beckoning Clara to come, to follow. Grabbing her things and covering the tiny fire with dirt, Clara followed.

The tiny figure bobbed and drifted side to side as it slowed to Clara's pace, leading her through the trees, taking an easy path for Clara to follow. The voice remained incomprehensible, but Clara felt that this tiny person must be leading her to a place where she could rest, perhaps a place where she could get shelter, water, food.

One flying woman became two, the second clad in leaves sewn together with the same silk. Then a third wearing flowers, then a fourth, and soon, Clara was surrounded by the tiny figures. The voices grew to a constant buzz, and delight filled the fifteen-year-old girl, until suddenly they all stopped moving forward and instead clustered in towards her. Closer, she saw these were not tiny women. They were strange, insect-like creatures, running silk strands from somewhere under their garments, wrapping Clara in a cocoon of threads so strong that she felt as if she were bound by wire. Then, she felt herself hoisted into the air, dangled from a branch.

Chapter 9

TREASURE SEEKERS

Karasta

There was no way to know which direction they were walking in, Peter thought as he followed the tiny red dragon. They couldn't even see the sky through the dense layer of leaves above them. Petunia seemed sure of herself, though. She sped ahead, and he was glad that the way at ground level was fairly open, save for fallen branches, as the amount of light was low and he was having a hard time keeping up with her.

"Slow down," he called out, and Petunia turned, hovering, her wings beating double time to keep her in one spot.

"Slow poke. Why can't you move faster?" she responded.

Peter stopped, bending down, panting from the exertion. "I'm almost running to keep up with you, and I can't see very well. If I step in the wrong place, I could break a leg. Do you even know where we're going?"

"Of course I do," Petunia responded. "The ground tugs me in the direction I need to go. It's like it says, 'North is that way,' so I know West is to the left of that pull, and East is to the right, and South is all the way in the other direction."

"That kind-of makes sense," mused Peter. "The planet has a magnet inside it, so it's no wonder you can feel it. Now you just need to explain to me how you know where the hoard is in relation to where we are."

"Oh. Um." Petunia looked confused. "Didn't we portal to the spot I showed you on the map?"

"Yes, but every millimetre on the map is many kilometres in real life. The spot I think you pointed out may be a long way away from where we need to be."

"That's okay then. I know exactly where we needed to go, and I trust you to put me there exactly."

Peter puffed out his cheeks. "That's a lot of trust. I'm not so sure I'm worthy of it."

"Don't worry." Petunia settled herself on Peter's shoulder. "Do you remember that time you made all the string? The brown string and the white string. And I helped."

"I remember your 'help'," Peter groused. "You got everything into a huge knot that took me ages to unravel."

"That's right! You and I are like that string, all tied up together. So where I want to go, you know too, even if you don't know you know."

"You're a little bit strange sometimes, do you know that?"

Petunia kissed him on the cheek. "I know. That's why you love me."

After Peter had convinced Petunia to move at a less hurried pace, he found that he was able to look around. He hadn't forgotten his mission to retrieve Pojeru fruit, so he started to take his time searching for the elusive vine. The first he came upon had only unripe fruit, the berry cluster within the delicate cape hard and green. The second vine held shiny, black berries inside the lacy cape, and so Peter tested his concept of stasis — a nothing place with only void. Unfortunately, the berry appeared to not enjoy being in a void; each drupelet swelled and exploded, spraying juice inside the cape, which then rolled down the sides and out the opening at the bottom.

"Ooh, instant juicing! That looks like a really good way to make drinks," Petunia remarked, flying loops in the air happily.

"I need to store them in stasis, not juice them," grumbled Peter. "I don't know what I did wrong. I put them into a nothing place so they couldn't oxidise."

"But don't you need to take them to a place without time so they can't change?" Petunia looked at him with a quizzical tilt of her head. "I thought that time was one of the things that made change happen."

Peter felt embarrassed the second she said that. Of course it was time. Not oxygen, not vacuum, not void. "You're right. I hadn't thought of stasis like that before. You're so smart."

"I know," Petunia said, happily, then zipped off to chase a bright yellow dragonfly while he worked it out.

Petunia was right. Peter found it hard to imagine a place with no time. He supposed it was like an insect stuck in amber, unable to change. Like a pendulum at the top of its swing, unable to drop. He pushed his mind into more abstract concepts of energy stilled, unable to alter its form, numbers creeping across his imagination, until suddenly it clicked.

Gently lifting a hand and pinching the stem between thumb and forefinger, he imagined stillness at the same time as the berry came away from the vine. It was hard, like steel, and an ant, which moments before had been trundling across the face of the fruit, was now unmoving. Peter tested the give in the cape, which should be feathery and light, but there was no flex. Breathing deeply, he pulled out a pouch from his backpack and dropped the fruit inside, hanging the pouch from his hip so he knew where it was.

With a smile of delight, he looked around for Petunia.

She wasn't there.

"Petunia," he called. "Where are you? It worked! You were right."

The sounds of the jungle stopped abruptly at his loud call. He listened intently, for a response, but the sounds of the birds, the insects, the soft movements in the underbrush, all started up again moments later without any return call.

"Where did you go to? Petunia!" he called again, setting out in the direction he had seen her trailing the dragonfly. Deep inside, he berated himself for letting her out of his sight. He should have been paying better attention. He should have been looking which way she was going.

He almost missed it because he was so busy telling himself he should have been paying attention. There, holding onto a stem of a fern, was a bright yellow… something. Now he was closer, he could see it wasn't a dragonfly, nor was it strictly yellow. More like a tiny feminine shape with dragonfly wings, glowing with yellow light. A memory tugged on him, of one of Scaramond's books he would pull out just to look at the pictures. It was this thing. It was a pyksee.

His blood ran cold in terror. *Archaeidae sapiens*. These were spiders, not insects. Social spiders that lived in vast colonies and were known to lure men into their midst. Where there was one, there must be a hundred or more, seeking to capture him and suck his vital juices.

The pyksee rose into the air on its gossamer wings that Peter knew were specialised legs, beckoning with the two arms that Peter knew weren't truly arms. It rubbed its legs together, legs that looked like they belonged on a slender, beautiful woman (if at a miniaturised scale), and the air was filled with the sound of almost voices, just at the edge of his hearing, as if someone were talking to him through a wall.

Peter thought about Petunia and wondered if the pyksees were interested in dragon blood. It was very different to mammalian blood, he knew, and he hoped this would keep the tiny dragon off the menu, but fearing the worst, he steeled his heart and followed the glowing spider as it flew through the trees.

More pyksees appeared around him the further he followed, and he cast his mind back to the first magic he ever used, suppressing the noise of his passage, being silent, stilling his presence, even as he continued following. He grew colder, but in the damp heat of the jungle, the cool was refreshing. Slowly the pyksees drifted away, but as the light faded, he continued in the same direction, hoping to come upon the mass of the colony.

A trickle of laughter floated through the trees, melodic and sweet—Petunia's laugh. Swifter, now, Peter ran towards the sound, only to see his friend playing a chasing game with the pyksees. Not just a couple—hundreds of them. They flew in loops and whirls, tracing intricate spirals of light in the air that were filled with beauty. Peter's breath stopped in his chest as he watched, mindful of the precarious situation he was in. He settled down to watch, and eventually Petunia settled, tired, and the pyksees settled alongside her.

"I wonder where Peter is," mused Petunia sleepily, and Peter took the opportunity to move, gathering the small dragon into his arms, wrapping her in his invisibility. He crept away from the pyksee colony, stopping only when he could no longer see the glow of their light.

"Why did we leave the delightful ladies," asked Petunia. "They were fun."

"They're dangerous," said Peter. "They may not want to eat you, but they'll make a meal out of me, or any other person who happens their way."

Hot on the heels of his words, faint screams drifted through the trees from back in the direction they had just come from.

"Sounds like I managed to hit that thought spot on the head," Peter said flatly. "Are you up to helping me rescue someone?"

"Of course. Nobody hurts my friends," said Petunia, "If you go in alone, you'll be eaten. Silly Peter, always being squishy and edible. It's like the entire world wants to kill you."

The pyksee colony was astir, not in the way it had been when Petunia had been flying with them, but in what looked like a whirlwind, flying in circles around a solid, struggling mass in the centre. It wasn't screaming anymore, though; the sounds had muffled to a buzzing "Mmph, mmph…," nearly drowned out by the susurrations of so many pyksees with their almost-speech.

Petunia flew up to investigate the struggling mass, breathing brief bursts of flame whenever the pyksees got in her way. They burned well, the high-pitched noises of their internal fluids squealing as they fell away in tiny flames. Reaching the top, a single burst of flame scattered the remaining arachnids as the threads anchoring the cocoon to the trees was severed and the wrapped form fell.

Peter rushed forward, cutting away the sticky threads from the girl before him. Heedless of the strands of web that still clung to him, he grabbed her by the hand. "We're going to run now."

Chapter 10

Bakar

Chance watched out of the study windows as Scaramond walked the grounds, gesturing, and for each hand movement, an entire building appeared.

Chance had always known that there was something there. Many somethings, all hidden away in dimensional pockets. Sometimes, when he walked the grounds, he would feel them there, pushing against reality and begging to be revealed, tickling the back of his throat with the unspoken words of release.

As his eighteenth birthday approached, Scaramond gave him increasingly more time to himself, as if there were no point in trying to oversee his progress at this point. Or perhaps it was just that Scaramond trusted him to do the work as he saw fit, and that he was considered able to conduct himself appropriately now that he was almost an adult. Whatever the reason, Chance felt a shiver of rebellion coursing through him as he realised that the vast grounds held untold opportunities to explore. So, after several tall buildings were exposed and his Master had disappeared between the red brick edifices, Chance left the books open on the table and ran down the stairs, out the door, and chose a new door at random.

A long, wide hallway greeted him, chairs along one wall, cubby holes on another wall, doors interspersed along the walls at regular intervals. Some doors were closed, others open, seemingly at the whim of whoever had been the last person to use the room. The cubbies weren't all empty—some held books, others held clothing—hats, jackets, scarves, one held a neat pair of shoes, as if their owners would return at any minute to retrieve them. Picking up a slate, Chance found that the owner had been taking notes on fluid dynamics—the motion of water and gases as they moved around the planet. He put it back down and investigated the rooms, one at a time.

These were classrooms. Writing desks filled the room in roughly parallel lines, each desk with a chair, some chairs pushed in neatly, others angled out or away from the desk, as if their occupants hadn't cared about how they left the furniture. The desks were covered in graffiti, carved deep into the surface or painted on in ink. D.W. woz ere. Hearts with names or initials inside. Insults, rude signs, swear words, all indelibly marked over years, decades maybe. Chance ran a curious finger over the letters, wondering about the people who left these marks. Lifting a creaky desktop, he found that it was not empty, containing half an apple that looked like it had only just been left, still fresh, if a little browned. He closed the lid and looked towards the large slate that covered almost the entirety of the wall at the end of the room. Someone had been marking intricate mathematical formulae in white chalk, discussing circles and ellipses, along with some other calculations he couldn't quite follow.

Each room along this side of the hall held a similar story, if a different class, different books, different table layout. Then, stepping through a door at the end of the hall, he found himself in a narrow room with a set of rickety stairs going up.

Chance surmised that this was a staff passage, especially when he found himself in a warren of tight offices and storage spaces. Some areas looked cleaner, more well used than others, and occasionally he found that the areas in good use had strange delights, such as the cup of cooling tea on one desk or the half-eaten pastry in another. But he was most curious about the faint sounds he heard while looking at the titles on a bookshelf in one room, as if someone was moving on the other side of the wall.

He muddled out the route in his head, realising that he couldn't find the noise from the passageway he was currently in, and backtracked slowly, looking for the room that would lie on the other side of that wall. Perhaps it was simply a curtain swinging in the breeze, but his curiosity was piqued, and he found himself traversing paths that were in varying states of disrepair. Deeper and deeper into the labyrinthine collection of rooms he went, finding storage rooms that were more bizarre than anything he had seen before, with desks and chairs piled high that held graffiti in unknown alphabets, books that seemed to be written in some kind of cipher that looked almost familiar but not quite.

Then, turning into a small closet, he found the source of the noise.

A small child, wearing jacket and pants in navy blue with yellow trim, was drawing pictures on the wall with a stick of chalk.

Chapter 11

Bakar

Felicity's feet crunched firmly in the gravel as she stepped onto the long parade that led to the tower. She hadn't been here before, but she was confident that she had followed Peter's instructions to the letter. She felt some hesitation, though, as she was sure that Peter had said there were only two buildings here, rather than the dozen or so that were arrayed pleasantly either side of the white gravel.

As she approached the tower that lay at the end of the drive, she relaxed. The tall form of Scaramond, dressed in his familiar red robes, stepped out of the door and awaited her. Her steps quickened and she felt a large grin appear across her face, recalling how on Peter's birthday, that day of such terror, the mage had been there to treat her with kindness. It helped, she thought, that he was so attractive.

"Greetings," Scaramond called out, "I offer you sanctuary that you might find respite. Rest and be filled."

Felicity fluttered a hand at her breast. "Why, Mr Mond, you do flatter a lady with your fancy ways, all traditional and that. You sound just like my grandpappy did whenever I visited. He gave me a little response to say and all. Now, what was it..." Felicity thought a moment, her eyes scrunched up. "Oh, yes! I remember. My thanks, gracious host. I bear good will and respect. I accept your offer in peace that I rest and be filled. Yes, that was it."

Scaramond smiled a secret, closed smile. "That's it perfectly, Mrs Diefen," he said with warmth. "The old ways were such courteous marvels, weren't they? We're in a much harsher time now, don't you think?"

"Oh, yes, Mr Mond, the past was so much more pleasant, I think. Nothing but ruffians out there nowadays. Excluding you, my dear Mr Mond, of course." Felicity placed a hand on Scaramond's arm, and he covered it with his own hand, turning to lead her to the front door.

"I'm afraid Peter isn't here right now," Scaramond's voice dropped to a low, conspiratorial tone as if he were sharing the secrets of the universe, "He and Petunia have gone on a mission to deepest, darkest Qoth. But," he said, brightening his tone, "I would delight in your company for some light refreshments, if I am a suitable replacement."

Felicity blushed, barely noticing the oddness of her surroundings as she looked at her feet shyly. "Oh, of course, Mr Mond. In fact, I was here to invite you to a morning tea. Well, not just you," she hastily added, blushing more fiercely, "But also Peter, and Petunia, and Misty, and Chance. I was going to say tomorrow, but if Peter and Petunia are away, I can wait for them to get back."

"I'm sure they will be as delighted to accept as I am. Just watch your step here." Scaramond helped her onto the moving stairway, and suddenly Felicity realised they were not in an ordinary room. She looked around her and gasped as they rose, the three-storeyed library dropping away behind her.

"I didn't know that there were this many books in the world!" she exclaimed.

Scaramond grinned at her. "This is just the ones on display," he confided. "I have others that people don't need to look at quite so often."

Felicity and Scaramond had only been chatting a few moments in the small parlour when Chance burst in, wild eyed, dragging a girl behind him. The girl looked scared and confused, and was babbling in a strange language that Felicity thought sounded a lot like the gobbling of turkeys.

Scaramond looked very startled, and spoke to the child in the strange gobbling language for several minutes, while Felicity took a chance to look at the child's strange clothing. Apart from the girl being dressed in trousers, there were other oddities to attire — unusual neckline, wide collar, and the patterning of those trousers, which Felicity could instantly imagine on the nobles of Bakar, flattering the hips and lengthening the look of the legs. *Yes,* Felicity thought, *If I could get some time to study those trousers, I could make the pattern distinctively mine.*

"This is a most unusual turn of events, Mrs Linter," Scaramond said, breaking Felicity's chain of thought. "It seems poor Yslt here has been in stasis since the last time I used one of the buildings over there." He pointed vaguely in the direction of the gardens to the front of the tower then rubbed his cheek in concern. "She knows not a lick of the language."

"Oh, my," said Felicity, tears welling in her eyes, "She's been trapped? The poor child!"

"Time hasn't passed for her at all, so no need to worry on that score."

"But her parents! They must be frantic with worry," said Felicity, imagining what the world would be like if Peter were missing. It was hard enough when he was safe but far away, but if she hadn't known if he was alright — that was a fear Felicity could barely comprehend.

"They, I'm afraid, are long since dead. There was a war, you see, and her parents were both combatants…"

"Oh, the poor mite. Who's to take care of you," Felicity asked, passing the child one of the violet-flavoured jellies from the selection of sweets before her. Yslt looked to Scaramond, who nodded, then greedily stuffed the stiff, cuboid jelly into her mouth happily.

"This used to be a school, and she was resident here before the school closed rather abruptly. There used to be staff to take care of her and all the other residents, but they are long gone. Obviously, I cannot take her in. I'm worried about the look of it - a bachelor such as myself raising a young girl who is not my relative. I just don't know what to do with her."

Felicity hesitantly offered the first solution in her head. "I... I could take her in. There would be no impropriety, and she is young enough that I could teach her how to sew... I cannot understand her language, though."

Scaramond leapt forward, clasping Felicity's hand and looking deep into her eyes. Felicity felt the heat rising once more and excitement filled her chest at his closeness. "I would be most grateful, Mrs Diefen. Of course, I will pay you a stipend to foster the child, and when the school reopens I would like her to attend classes, but you would be doing me the most wonderful of services. She is young, she must learn the language, there is no need for you to learn hers."

"Yes, yes, Mr Mond, I will be very glad to foster this girl. Eselt, did you call her? Yes, I will provide her the best of care."

Chapter 12

Bakar

The Headmaster had explained to Yslt that there had been a student gathering hyn had missed. That students had all been sent home. That hyn had been stored in a stasis bubble for a long time. That Nanny Triph was no longer available and that the language in Bakar was different, so hyn had to learn a new language now.

Yslt asked about hyn friends, but Headmaster Skaraman said they were all gone away. Headmaster Skaraman talked in a strange language like chickens clucking to the person in the fluffy clothing. The fluffy-clothed person watched hyn like an eagle watched chicks, looking at their body. Yslt didn't like the way they were looking at hyn, but Headmaster Skaraman seemed to think this was alright. Then, the Headmaster told Yslt to go with the fluffy person.

The strange, fluffy person couldn't even get their name right, Yslt thought. "Eselt," the fluffy person called hyn, grabbing hyn by the hand and pulling hyn away from Headmaster Skaraman's house. Yslt had looked around and seen that many of the buildings were missing, and that the plants had all changed.

Bakar was different. Bigger, perhaps. The streets had rounded cobbles rather than the red dirt that had been there before. Houses were ugly, square and made of wood, rather than the rounded yurts of colourful fabric that hyn recalled. It was almost like these people lived here year round, rather than making an annual pilgrimage to the site. How could anyone stay here? The war made it impossible to gather more than a few in any one place permanently, Yslt thought, then shrugged it off as one of the Headmaster's many mysteries.

"Kam, Eselt," clucked the fluffy person. Hyn looked at the outstretched hand and decided that it must mean that hyn should take it and follow. Hyn took it. The hand felt dry and strange, like leather that had been boiled a long time without proper stretching, so now it was furrowed and unpleasant. Hyn could feel calluses on the tips of the fluffy person's fingers. This must be how the fluffy person managed with so much clothing, Yslt thought. Perhaps hyn only worked with hyn fingers, and so never needed to move. Yslt tried to imagine being encased in so much cloth, but couldn't envision it — it seemed so strange.

Yes, Bakar was much changed. The rope bridge that once made way over churning waters had been replaced with a sturdy wooden structure that was wide enough for an entire herd of cattle. Hyn thought that the river was quieter then hyn had ever seen it, too, and hyn wondered how that had happened, but before hyn had a chance to ask, they were already past the river.

The place they were approaching seemed a lot safer than the wood places, thought Yslt. It was a big tent, large enough for three families, white, as if it wanted to hide during snows, with little vines and flowers sewn into canvas. Yslt could feel the smile on hyn face bursting out, and hyn wanted to run in and explore, meet all the people who must be waiting inside, but the hard hand was there and Yslt waited like Nanny Triph would have expected.

But inside, there was nobody. The rugs were nice, but the walls were hard, like in the school. There were no floor cushions, only high seats and tables and cupboards and things.

The fluffy person sat Yslt down and pointed. "Yu, Eselt. Mea, Flisitty."

Yslt tried to say the person's name, but the strange words wriggled in hyn mouth like a small fish. Finally, hyn settled on a close sound. "Yu, Yslt. Mea, Flif-sifty."

The look on the strange Sifty person's told Yslt that there was something wrong with what hyn said, but Yslt filed the name away. *Close,* Nanny Triph often said, *was better than not trying at all.*

Chapter 13

Qoth/Karasta Border

The catafalque moved slowly south to the border, never stopping. At intervals, a new soldier would be dispatched to take the place of another in pulling the caisson, allowing the soldiers to eat and rest on the horse-drawn wagons that followed.

Hrodolf occasionally stepped out of his carriage to walk amongst the subjects who milled around, or stepped back to quietly chat with some of the nobles, many of whom had managed to hurriedly dig out black garments for the event. He found this part of the journey especially boring, but late night conversations with his military advisors had his mind tumbling in a mix of excitement, anticipation, and trepidation. Seeing the mass of his army following behind, ostensibly as a show of respect for the deceased, stiffened his spine proudly.

The problem of Qoth had been preying on his mind for some time. The civil war in Qoth seemed like an opportunity. The death of their Queen had left the leadership non-existent. Their succession was uncertain, with no clear heir. But up until now, he hadn't known how to leverage the situation. This Em, this strange lobster-like creature, was the pivot upon which the strong arm of his Karastan force could move the rigid load of his Southern border.

And so, he endured the maddeningly slow pace, one step at

a time.

He looked over to the strange Magus who had walked the entire journey so far, his hand on the bier. Hrodolf wondered if he planned to remain like that the entire journey, which was likely to last several days, or if he intended to take rest stops at some point. Returning to his carriage, he leant over to Colton.

"Make certain the Magus is being offered food and drink at regular intervals. The man hasn't stopped once, I believe. Insanity. A man of his status shouldn't be walking like a commoner. Let him know that there is a space to rest here."

Colton nodded and left the confines of the carriage, returning a few moments later.

"The Magus is refusing all food and drink. I've left instructions that it be offered to him on the half hour from hereon out. Additionally, he has refused rest. He plans to walk the entire way without sleep, apparently. Cited words he said were from the previous Magus: 'Magus simply means mage. The Magus is not Arch, not High, not King nor Emperor. The Magus is no better than any other. The Magus is, in fact, a servant. He (or she) serves all of Varthien.' He says he is giving service to Em and to Wamanil clan by being her escort home.

"I also believe he may be serving the rest of us by keeping the carcass—I mean corpse—cold. There was a distinct chill in the air as I approached. I think that is a great boon to us all, as I have smelt the garbage remains of Chirren on a hot day. It's one of the least pleasant scents I can imagine."

"His choice, I suppose," Hrodolf shrugged. "At least most of this road is cobbled. I can't imagine how hard it must be on his feet. No shoes? The man dresses like a pauper. How does he expect to curry goodwill if he's not dressed correctly?"

"I suppose he expects the respect granted him by the office," Colton said with the flat tone in his voice that he often used when he thought Hrodolf was being an idiot.

Two days later, the catafalque was still moving, and Magus

Linter was moving with it, a step at a time. An unbelieving Hrodolf had questioned soldiers who had been stationed as the Catafalque Party during those hours, but each confirmed that Magus Linter had remained by the bier the entire time.

Hrodolf himself had been less inclined to discomfort, and each evening sent servants to set up his pavilion ahead of their progress, so that he might pass the night in an actual bed, then caught back up to the convoy in the morning. Most nobles chose to do the same, with many dropping off as time went by, until today, when none were left save those who were duty bound as his military officers. He didn't blame them. The slow progress was mind-numbing and if he'd had a chance, he would be home right now.

"Fetch Farrar for me, Colton. I want to know what to expect when we reach the border."

The wait for Farrar was, as usual, somewhat longer than Hrodolf would normally tolerate, but he supposed the man did have a fair amount of responsibility and was due a little leeway. However, the look of anxiety on Farrar's face as he entered the carriage sent a bolt of panic through the king.

"What is it, man? You look like you've just lost half the army. Are we in battle already?"

"No, Majesty, there's been no fighting yet. We're still about an hour from the border. But a personal problem has arisen. I've just received word from my home estate. Someone claims to have taken my daughter and is demanding a ransom. They provided Clara's travel papers as proof of capture."

"The timing is suspicious, considering that we've got so many forces on the move right now. Do you think this may be a ploy to split your focus?"

"Perhaps, Majesty. Clara was definitely on the road from her mother's estate in Southern Qoth, and she's been extraordinarily late arriving. There was no word of her retinue, and only the paperwork acting as proof. I have sent word back to my people to send a small party with the messenger, carrying the ransom amount without giving it directly to him, but to follow carefully with a larger party to attempt capture of the crew. Meanwhile, there is nothing I can do directly, so my focus is on the coming troop movements.

"If these Wamanil chirren accept our legitimacy as their rulers, we can redraw the border straight away with them at our backs, but immediate human nobility may have a bit of a tantrum about that and claim that animals don't count as allies. Let's send an envoy to Titingarn. He's got a stake in the conflict—first cousin I believe? Plus he's distant. Southern border. If we tell him you're supporting his claim, we can send in our peacekeeping force under his banner and give us a greater amount of legitimacy, plus allow us to squeeze the others between the two forces."

"Titingarn. I think I remember him. Vapid sort of man, no fun at parties, just wants to talk about his pigeons? He'll do. Easily led. I once told him that our toy poodles had been full sized but someone left them out in the rain and they shrank. Perfect to place into power."

"I'll get the pigeoneer onto sending the message—should stroke Titingarn's ego nicely if he gets a few of his birds back."

The border was quiet here. A couple of bored sentries stood at the Karastan outpost, but the Qoth outpost stood empty, its door open and swinging slightly in the wind.

At the approach of the army, the sentries trotted out and stood sharply to attention, the Captain stepping forward and saluting.

General Farrar walked up, inspecting the men, then turned to the Captain. "Report."

"Thu… the Qoth locals abandoned their outpost a week or so back, sir. Um, we had, um we…" His eyes drifted over the large number of people behind the General, and he licked his lips nervously.

"Eyes on me, man. Don't look at them."

The captain swallowed heavily, then fixed his gaze once more on General Farrar. "We had a few local layabouts come check out the Qoth outpost and loot what had been left behind, but they didn't approach us, sir. Nor no refugees, sir."

"No refugees? You'd think they would be more than you could handle here."

"Not this post, sir. The road east of here prob'ly got most of 'em. The Qoth road south here is bad. Washes out several times a year. The local toff doesn't see fit to upkeep it. It's mostly quiet a'cos of that."

"Any scouts?"

"We see people sometimes, but they don't bother with us, and so long as they stay that side, we don't bother with them."

Farrar nodded, then turned to Hrodolf. "Probably safe, but from here we'll be in enemy territory. Keep your royal guard close."

Hrodolf eyed the road ahead. "We hold here for a few minutes, I'll address the company." He turned to face his people.

"The way forward on our sojourn is Qoth. Our duty is one of one of peace and remembrance, not one of war. We seek today to protect, not to prey upon others. As we take these steps, we do so in love, love for our fellow man, love for people of all forms. As we go forth, tell all you encounter that King Hrodolf of Karasta, with Highlord Magus Linter by his side, bids that they set down arms against each other. We come not as agents of war but as agents of order and right, both in this funeral convoy, and in support of the one true king of Qoth, Lance Titingarn. All are welcome under his arms.

"Let us commence!" Hrodolf, a hand held majestically in the air, turned and led his people across the border, behind the ever-moving catafalque that had not paused to take in the King's words. Norman never once reacted, simply moving one bloody foot in front of the other, his sun-seared hand resting on the raised platform.

From here, the road to Wamanil clan branched off from the main thoroughfare and became more like a track. Tall trees blocked out the sun, and at times the catafalque needed to find a more suitable route where the caisson was wider than the passage through the trees would allow. Hrodolf was annoyed when Colton suggested that they needed to leave his carriage behind, but when he saw how thick the trees had become, he reluctantly agreed, thankful that the Chirren had chosen to build their settlement so close to the river that defined Karasta's southern border.

The way was mostly downhill, and he stepped carefully, his heeled shoes prone to catching on the branches and roots that lay beneath the fallen leaves. He despaired at the lace that adorned his cuffs, as stray branches and vines that seemed to have tiny, hooked claws grasped and clutched at him, tearing at the delicate fabric. He watched the Magus in bewilderment as the man moved through the trees with seeming ease, never stopping, a juggernaut, expecting the world to bend to him rather than give way to anything before him. After an hour, Hrodolf started to wince at the pain of each step, certain that his feet would soon be as raw and bleeding as those of the Magus. These were certainly not the shoes he would have chosen if he had expected to be hiking in the jungle, but, he supposed, he would never choose to go hiking in the jungle so he had no idea which shoes he would prefer.

When the catafalque finally broke through the wall of green, Hrodolf almost wept. Here would be civilisation once more.

Qoth

Peter and Clara ran, then walked, then ran, the entire night. The small dragon that was Peter's companion flew, or rode on a shoulder, occasionally scouting either side of where they were going, or checking ahead, or looking for pursuit. Clara had no idea which direction they were heading in, only that they hadn't stopped since Peter had grabbed her by the hand and said, "We're going to run now."

She was glad they hadn't stopped. She didn't want to stop. She was afraid that if they stopped, she would suddenly realise that she was still covered in that web, still struggling to breathe or move, being wrapped head to toe in the sticky gauze. She didn't want to slow down. She wanted to put as much distance as she could between her and her attackers.

Conversation was minimal and whispered. Enough that Petunia had introduced herself, then introduced Peter, and Clara had given her name, but not much more than that other than Petunia's occasional updates about the path ahead.

The way was utterly dark, and Clara thought it a wonder that neither she nor Peter had broken an ankle or had a major fall, though she did concede that there were a few places she had cuts or bruises from the vegetation, and perhaps there was a leech or two stuck to her neck or legs. It was all fine, so long as there was nothing that looked like a yellow, glowing dragonfly.

It was only when the world started to brighten about them that they finally started to slow themselves.

"I think…," puffed Peter, "I think… they may be… gone."

Clara sank against a wide tree trunk, nodding her head. "Yes. Thirsty now."

She rolled her head to the side, looking for any of the wide-leaved plants that she had previously used to collect dew. Groaning, she rolled onto her side to reach down for one nearby.

"Hold on," said Peter. "I know this one." Breathing deep and slow, he closed his eyes.

Clara watched in astonishment as streams of water rose from the surrounding plants, coming to meet as a single airborne tentacle. It undulated towards her, allowing her to sip directly from the source. Then, when she had her fill, it made its way to Peter's lips, then to Petunia. Finally, when all had their fill, the streams of water separated again, and slowly sank once more to the places they had arisen.

"What was that?" she asked.

"Peter's a wizard," said Petunia. "He can do anything."

"Anything?" Clara looked at Peter, an eyebrow raised.

Petunia piped up again. "Absolutely anything! He's amazing. He's the most best wizard in Varthien. He's the greatest. Peter the Greatest." She zipped around in spirals, diving into the bushes to scare the ground-nesting birds.

"If he's the greatest, why didn't he magic us away from evil dragonfly people instead of making us run all night?"

Petunia landed on a log, looking at Peter.

Peter looked ashamed. "I honestly didn't think of it," he admitted. "I haven't really been able to do many active effects for very long, and I just… I guess I just forgot I could do stuff?"

Petunia rolled her eyes. "Why didn't you tell me you forgot you could do magic? I would have reminded you. I never forget anything. I thought maybe you were having fun. You like running for fun sometimes. I remember times when you and Chance would go running and nothing was chasing you, and you did that for fun. You're weird like that sometimes."

"There's a difference between foot racing and running away from danger, Petunia."

"Great, well can you take us somewhere safe that's not in the middle of nowhere now?" Clara asked.

"I can, but I need some berries first."

"Oh, didn't you get all those yesterday?" Petunia asked. "There's some over there, near the beach." She pointed with her tail.

"Near the beach? There's a beach?" Clara asked, surprised. She hadn't thought they were so close to the coast. She stood, trudging with tired legs towards where Petunia had pointed, then parting the greenery, she saw the clear blue sky, the white sand, and between them, the darkness of the sea. "There's a beach!" she yelled back at Peter, and strode forward toward the sea, planning on dipping her aching bones into the cool water. She waded out into the waves, intent only on what was ahead of her, then turned to look back towards where she had left the other two.

It was only then that she saw what she had walked right past. Jumping and hollering at Peter, she yelled "There's a town!"

Chapter 15

Wamanil Clan

Hominids south, Chk thought. The younglings had seen them first, playing their hide and dig so well that the hominids had not noticed them.

Chk hurried along the pathways. Hominids could be nice or not, depending on factors that Chk had spent a lifetime learning.

Clan stepped out of his way, signalling the sign of respect as they did. Chk barely noticed this anymore. Wamanil's prosperity had become a thing he expected now, as easy as Father Sky and as fluid as Mother Water.

He stepped smoothly through the lush green around Wamanil edge, and there indeed were the hominids, two of them, one large and wearing a winged thing on its shoulder and one small, carrying a staff with an unusual top and wearing the holy colour of Father Sky from just below its head all the way to the ground. Its garb must signify rank, he thought. Approaching the smaller, he opened his arms in greeting, dropping his chelipeds in the sign of reverence.

The smaller hominid gave the wail of dolphins, stepping behind the large one and clutching its body. Chk stopped. Perhaps he had broken some protocol. He stood, arms outstretched, chelipeds still and unaggressive.

The large one moved its mouth. This meant the large one was trying to communicate, but Chk had never determined what the mouth movements meant specifically. Perhaps it was simply that Mother Water had not blessed these hominids with the power of speech. They lived far from her, and speech was always more difficult away from her embrace.

Chk beckoned with his arms. The large one turned and embraced the small one, then he turned back to face Chk and spread his arms in greeting. Chk pitied the hominids. They lacked the chelipeds that would bring them closer to Father Sky and Mother Water — they would never be able to make the sign of reverence. How they could ever approach civilisation or even manage simple tasks with only two arms always astounded him. Chk motioned for them to follow, to join him.

The large one held the end of the small one's arm, making more mouth movements in the small one's direction. Then they followed, the small one huddling behind the large one. Chk approved. It was right that one wearing the holy colour be protected.

Chk led them through the pathways, warning all he encountered to step aside. Some, however, could not restrain themselves, reaching out with their chelipeds to touch the soft fabric in the holy colour, and each time they did so, the small hominid would once again voice the dolphin wail and clutch its larger protector. Each time, he was forced to rebuke the guilty, clicking a cheliped in the sign of sin.

They came in due course to the round, and craftspeople immediately came to offer their wares to the hominids. He had seen no sign that these two bore trade items, other than the winged thing. Perhaps it was worn as a tribute to Father Sky? He had heard the younglings say that the smaller one had been communing with Mother Water when they first saw it, so perhaps these two were on a holy pilgrimage.

"Gift, don't sell," he said to Clan. "These two have holy purposes. They are in the service of Mother Water and Father Sky. See the staff the small one bears! It holds the stone that calls

Father Sky's wrath. Bring them food and drink, prepare places of rest. We must give them aid and succour."

Gifts were laid at the feet of the two, and gradually the smaller one seemed to relax. When food was brought to the two, the larger one ate first, offering morsels to the smaller to try. It appeared that it was acting in homage to the smaller, who must be the holier of the two. Only when the larger one had tried the food did the smaller eat. Perhaps the larger acted as a servant as well as a protector, considered Chk. This was not unusual in the world of hominids, who had a complicated power structure that differed depending on which coast they inhabited.

The two were then offered the Slings of the Father to rest in, strung between trees next to the Mother's Flow. No pallet close to the ground for them, he thought in triumph. He settled himself in guard as the two lay down to sleep, the winged thing settling on the large one's chest.

The Father's Eye was starting to close when younglings came again to report more hominids, east this time. Chk was torn. Protect the ones on pilgrimage or approach the new hominids? But the new hominids posed an unknown threat which could upset the holy two, so his mind was swiftly made up — he would assess the new arrival and leave these two in the bosom of Wamanil, trusting that Clan would neither harm nor harass the sleeping.

The pathways to the east were harder to navigate. They all moved uphill, further from Mother Water's calming embrace, working their way to the forsaken lands. Clan to the east were poorer, less capable. They lived in the grip of the green, Mother Water's colour, but this was the green of land growth, not the green of good sea grass. It was bright, like algae on still water, where the Mother's gift died. The eastern pathways were thick and choked; fewer feet walked these paths.

When he came to the place of the hominids, he stopped. There stood the Magus, who he had embraced as family just four of the Father's gazes prior. The Magus stood with a wooden wheeled thing, the thin scent of death and rot floating from its contents. Behind the magus stood the many. As many hominids as he had ever seen in one place. They each carried slivers of the Father's Stone, and he trembled at the thought of the wrath they could call. But the Magus was Clan. He stretched out his arms and dropped his chelipeds in the sign of respect.

"Welcome, Clan. And welcome to your guests."

The Magus lifted weary eyes to him. They were stained with the Mother's Gift. "I come in sorrow, Chk. Em has died at the hands of humans. I have brought her back to the body of Wamanil that she may be given a farewell within the Clan. This leader from the human tribe has joined me, seeking to show her the respect due, and has promised to stop his people from hunting Chirren."

A hominid near the Magus poked him in the shoulder and opened its mouth. The Magus moved his head up and down, then said "This leader would like to join with Wamanil, extending his protection to encompass your lands and defend Wamanil from other human tribes. Is this acceptable to Wamanil Clan?"

Chk thought, then spoke. "This is acceptable. We thank you for bringing her essence back to Wamanil. We must call all Clan to share in Em, that her creativity be spread once more among our people. Come, we have two on a holy pilgrimage who should meet with you. They will surely be grateful to share in Em and spread their love of Mother Water and Father Sky to your friends."

Chapter 16

NOURISHMENT

Wamanil Clan

Shadows crept in at the edges of Norman's vision, forcing him to move through a dark tunnel. He found his eyes closing at times like his eyelids were weights, and he would walk, eyes closed, until a toe found a rock and they popped open once more. Strange ghosts flickered in the periphery of his gaze, mumbling things that might have been real but probably existed only in the hidden passages of his mind. His conversation with Chk drifted like a dream, unexamined, a liminal space.

A vague awareness of meeting someone pulled him toward the sea, a great beast beside him with wheels and legs and heads, the child Em riding on its back, riding on the cold cloud of Norman's concern. She slept there, and he was bringing her closer, ever closer, home. Chk walked before him, showing him the way, bringing her back to family and warmth and love.

The days until now had been hard ones. He had been beset by visions of Albert lying on his death bed, of Felicity as her cheeks grew hollow, of Peter turning his back, of Petunia leaving, and always, always, of Em; her, holding the basket to him; her, gleefully showing off her new beads to friends; her, quartered, blue blood dripping over his hands; her, floating white chunks in a pink, creamy broth. He couldn't eat. He couldn't sleep. But he could walk, one step at a time, to bring her back to Wamanil clan.

Back to family. Back to her Mother and Father.

The warmth of the sun suffused his body, holding him in its radiance. Every shadow he passed through chilled him, like some great love being removed from his life, and he was beset with loss once more, but then he would pass once more into light and it would hold him in joy once more. He could feel the tears flowing, just as they had for days now, for Em, for Albert, for Felicity, for Peter and Petunia, for the losses of light and warmth and the joy when it returned.

Like a dream, a vision of Peter and Petunia swam before his eyes, him lying, suspended between pillars of brown and green, Petunia on his chest, the two together as if in death as they had always been in life. But no, Peter and Petunia weren't dead, were they? This must be a dream, like he had found himself in so many times since the start of his journey, but there was Chk, rushing toward them, and they rose. But Chk was not rushing to the two, he was rushing to a girl, cornflower blue dress, wavy, sun-bleached brown hair that whipped around her face in the wind, and Chk was bowing to her like she was some young goddess between the water and the sky. Peter and Petunia rose to their feet beside the blue goddess, and for the first time on this trek, Norman's hand fell from the bier beside him. Em was home.

The clan surrounded him, filing past the bier, each dipping a cheliped into the body, bringing it to their mouth, stuffing in a piece of white flesh, chewing voraciously. Then Chk came to him, passing him a piece of white flesh from Em's body.

"Eat with Wamanil, Magus. Be family."

Chapter 17

Wamanil Clan

The man's entire demeanour alarmed Clara. From the matted strands of gingery hair that whipped in the wind, to the undyed kaftan — dirty, stained under the armpits, the hem caked in mud and torn. The strange Chirren that had led her here pushed a piece of white meat into the man's mouth; he complied like a child, chewing mindlessly.

"Is he alright," she asked, but Peter was staring at the man with an open mouth, and Petunia was doing her backflips again. Clara reluctantly stepped forward.

"Are you alright," she repeated, directing her question to the man himself this time.

His gaze followed her, head moving instead of his eyes, as if he were hypnotised. He swayed to some unheard song, his intense gaze under bushy brows staring unblinking at her. Uncomfortable with the eye contact, Clara dropped her gaze. His feet were bare and bloody, as if he had walked over shards of glass.

"Let's get you lying down," she said, leading him to the hammock she had just deserted. "You look like you need to lie down."

Peter followed the two, still silent. He watched the man carefully. Clara wasn't sure what was going on, but at least Peter wasn't watching her anymore.

She turned back to the people that were following in the man's wake and was startled to realise that the man leaning with one hand on a nearby hut and looking at something on the sole of his shoe looked remarkably like the woodcut she'd studied at home of King Hrodolf. She tugged absently on Peter's sleeve to get his attention, then hurried up to the man.

Long hours of deportment studies had prepared her for this moment, and she curtseyed deeply, her head low and gazing at the ground. "Your most royal majesty," she started, "I am deeply humbled… um, honoured… to be in your most royal presence…" The words tumbled out of her mouth in a rush, strangely garbled as if her tongue was trying to twist itself into knots. She bobbed in place in the curtsey, still looking down, not quite certain how long she should hold it and feeling like perhaps she was stretching the time out too long, but unwilling to look up in case she didn't curtsey long enough. She racked her brains trying to remember, but all she could think of was the switch that had followed when she dropped the curtsey incorrectly.

"Ah. A subject!"

Clara swallowed and took this as a reason to rise.

"My blasted heel is loose." The king shook it under her nose, as if this was going to be important. Clara stared at it, seeing that, indeed, the heel was twisting and had come away slightly from the sole.

"Is there a cobbler anywhere in this blasted place? I had to leave my carriage back there…" he waved a hand vaguely at the jungle behind him, "…and how am I going to do anything with a loose heel?"

"Um," Clara bobbed her head at the king, feeling somewhat like a pigeon. She couldn't seem to stop—every time she looked up, she felt like she needed to bow. "I don't know. Perhaps you could just bang the heel on a rock or something."

"Bang my heel on a rock? Are you mad? I'm not an animal!"

Hrodolf looked over Clara's shoulder. "Oh, an animal. It's

one of those Chirren things. There's an awful lot of them here, aren't there?"

"Yes. I think this is one of their towns."

"One of their…? Oh. Yes. Right. One of their towns." King Hrodolf straightened up, putting his shoe back on, loose heel and all. "What is that you're waving at me? It looks like raw crab. I don't eat raw crab."

"I think it's from the big box…" Clara looked downhill, towards the beach, where chirren were milling around.

"Oh. Ew. No, I definitely don't want any of…" King Hrodolf was leaning backwards, away from the waving cheliped one moment, and the next had a mouthful of raw meat in his mouth. He chewed and swallowed.

"Savages. That's one of their own, there. And here's me, I've just issued a proclamation against eating these blasted creatures, and yet they're there forcing it down our bloody throats? What is that damn Magus playing at? Where is he? Oh, wait, is that him down there?"

Not waiting for an answer, the King strode past Clara and toward the beach. She started to follow, but stopped abruptly at a voice from the tree line.

"Clara?"

Clara turned back to the trees, scanning carefully. She almost missed him against the dark spaces between the trees, his dark leather breastplate drawing in the light, but then she saw him moving.

"Father?" Clara was hesitant. She hadn't seen him in several years, and she mistrusted her memory of his face, but this face was familiar, was him, the voice hard but sparking a warmth inside her.

Farrar Angmeyer stepped out towards her, searching her face. "It is you, isn't it? Gods, you have grown so much. Let me look at you." Rather than looking at her, he took her into a big embrace, one arm around her waist, the other cradling her head.

"They said you'd been kidnapped," he mumbled into her

hair. "I could hardly think, I was so worried. Gods, there's going to be a war, a big one, and your mother should have sent you over the mountains, not to me. What are we going to do?"

Clara could feel the warm wetness of his tears tickling her on the ear. She awkwardly patted his sides with her trapped arms. "I'm okay, I did what you taught me. I remembered how to shim..." she pulled away from him to grab the butterknife from her waistband. Holding it up for him to see, she said, "It was so nice and thin, and the shackle came off, and then I could climb out."

A big grin spread across Farrar's face, into his eyes, crinkling the corners.

"And then I remembered to follow the land, try to find the rivers, but there were these things, strange tiny ladies with wings," Farrar's face dropped, but Clara continued, "And they pulled me up in the air, but my friend and his pet dragon rescued me..."

"I am not a pet!" Petunia's voice sang loud in Clara's ear. "I come to tell you that Norman's sleeping now, and here you are, telling people I'm a pet." Petunia hovered carefully in front of Farrar, her long tail wrapped up in a spiral like a seahorse. "Hi, I'm Petunia. Who are you? You're not being mean to my Clara, are you?"

"No, Petunia, this is my father," Clara replied, interrupting Farrar's indrawn breath. "He's not mean to me."

"You have a father? You didn't tell me you had a father. We have Norman, and Peter, and you, and me, and now your father and we can have a big party! And we can invite all your friends, Mr Clara's Father!"

"Friends?" Clara peered into the trees.

Farrar cleared his throat. "Yes. My... friends... are setting up places for camp. I've told them to not harass the local Chirren population, and to avoid stripping all of the edibles from the area. I was just on my way to report when I found you."

"Oh. Oh-h-h-h-h." Clara suddenly realised what 'friends'

meant. "So, there really is a bigger war?"

"I'm here, and this is Qoth, so it's going to get ugly."

"I'm in Qoth? I didn't realise I'd crossed the border again. Wow. If we crossed the border just running away from, what were they, Petunia?"

"Pyksees."

"Right. Running away pyksees, there's got to be other people just crossing the border wherever they want."

"Border control is a difficult matter. You are right, of course. It's one of the reasons we're here. Hrodolf wants a bigger slice of the pie so, sooner or later, all of those refugees will be Karastan citizens and it won't really matter where they came from. Pyksees, you say? I'll need a rough location, then I'll send pigeons. We'll need those burned out. Can't have pyksees eating our people. Bad for citizen morale."

"I can show you on a map," said Petunia. "I'm good with maps. Maps are like looking at things from in the sky, only bigger and not as blue. Peter and Clara thought we were lost, but I always know where I am."

"That sounds like a handy skill to have," Farrar said in a measured voice. His face held a non-threatening smile. "Maybe you can be my navigator when you grow up."

"That would be fun. I can do it now. I'm big. I used to be little, but now I'm much bigger." Petunia puffed herself up pridefully, unfurling her long, red tail.

"I can see how big you are," said Farrar. "You need to be a little bigger for my army though. Let's go down to the beach now. I need to talk to my King."

Clara walked down to the beach once more. Everything hurt. Her feet, her legs, her back, her arms. It had been nice to rest for a while on the hammock, but she hadn't really felt comfortable, and the sun had been in her eyes, so she still felt like she hadn't slept in a long time. It was nice to have Father here though. She had felt unsafe around the Chirren — they looked so alien—but Father's presence was a little ball of safety that she could crawl inside. He would keep her safe. Nothing bad would happen now that he was here.

Peter was there, sitting by the hammock she had led the man to—Norman, she recalled Petunia call him. He was gently rocking the hammock as if its inhabitant were a baby and not a grown man. A large conch filled with murky, red-brown water sat by him, a sponge resting within. Norman's feet were clean now, and Clara surmised that Peter must have washed them, checking for how deep the lacerations were or whether there was infection.

As she approached, Peter looked up. The worried look on his face became a large smile, his eyes crinkling in happiness. "How are you? Recovered from last night?"

"I am, mostly," she said. "It's kind of like a dream, or like it all happened to someone else. How about you?"

Peter flexed his muscles. "I'm good. I like bushwalking. It was a little unexpected to be running all night, but I'm just glad to have found you. Who are those others you were talking to?"

Clara leaned in and pointed. "The man with all the lace is King Hrodolf of Karasta, and the man talking to him is General Farrar Angmeyer, my Father."

"Your dad. Your dad is here. How is your dad here? I don't get it. And Norman. How is Norman here? Norman's supposed to be in Pugton, not on the other end of the continent."

"Who is this Norman? You know him, I take it."

"I apprenticed under Norman. He's the Magus now, but he wasn't when I was his apprentice. Petunia knows him too. It's really strange that he's right here, right now."

Petunia flitted over at the sound of her name, catching the tail end of what Peter said. "You remember that brown and white string?"

"String?"

"Yes. I told you about it yesterday. You and I are the tangled string. But your string is also tangled up with Norman's string, and it's a different colour. It can be — um — green? Yes, he can be green string. Your brown string and my white string are tangled, and your brown string and Norman's green string are tangled in a different way. It's like the little bits of magic in you are all buzzing together, and they buzz together even when you're in different places."

"Wait, I think this sounds familiar. What was it called… quantum entanglement? Some book on the really deep magical phenomena was talking about it."

"That sounds like a mage-y way of saying what I just said."

"So you think I'm entangled with Norman at a quantum level. That sounds… awkward."

While Peter and Petunia argued about strange magical terms, Clara looked at the Magus. It looked like his beard was askew, and a piece of wire was sticking out above his ear. She put a hand out and gently lifted the wire, gasping as his face suddenly shifted under her hand, the jawbone softening, the cheek becoming more angular. Deep furrows criss-crossed the white skin where the fine metal had cut its way into the mage's flesh, or perhaps where the flesh had grown around the wire. The wire frame she now held in her hand looked nothing like the beard that had previously sat on Norman's face, a face that now looked feminine, and a body that now looked fuller of figure. Some of the wires were broken or twisted, and there were strange tufts of sheep's wool caught in the joins. She reached out to grab a tuft of wool, trying to untangle it from the frame.

Peter noticed the movement, and hurried to grab the wire frame.

"He gets really self-conscious about the way he looks, so don't ever touch that again. In fact, don't ever mention that you've seen him without his beard."

As Peter tenderly fitted the frame back over the Magus' ears, Clara noticed wires bending, untwisting, becoming straighter, rejoining. When both sides of the frame were safely tucked over Norman's ears, his beard looked cleaner, fuller, neater than it had before.

"You're really magic, aren't you," Clara asked. She had known before, but this cemented the knowledge in place. She felt somewhat nervous about the realisation, but then Peter looked at her through long eyelashes with a shy smile.

"Yeah. I suppose. I've never really thought about it."

Petunia popped up in front of Clara's face, breaking her eye contact with Peter. "I told you last night. He's the most best. Except maybe Norman. Norman's the boss of all the mages." She spun in the air. "What do you think, Peter? Are you better, or is Norman?"

"I think it really doesn't matter," Peter said. "It's not a competition." He stood and walked away, towards the table of food the Chirren had put out for their guests.

Petunia forlornly watched him walking away. "But, competitions are fun," she said, quietly.

Chapter 18

Bakar

Scaramond found himself once more in Misty's chamber, sitting in silence as she crooned her lullabies. The wooden chair creaked slightly as he shifted his weight to lean across the table and choose a different book.

"What are you reading this time, Scarred One?"

Misty's voice had returned, her tongue fully healed and nimble as a wyrmling's, courtesy of the metals Scaramond had gifted her. Hearing the full range of the draconic tones floated Scaramond in a bliss of nostalgia.

"A friend of mine wrote this, back in the day," he said. "'Tales of Merethien'. It's a collection of human folk tales, specifically from the isle, that popped up after the Shattering. Strange things. They attributed the Shattering to various gods, and if you really dig into it, you can identify which Mageunt is which god."

"It sounds fascinating. Would you read me some, sometime?"

He felt a warmth he hadn't felt in a long time, a comradeship. "Of course. I will find some suitable tales and..." He hissed in pain.

Deep in the bowels of the planet, Orange Skies thrashed in displeasure. While she wasn't able to know his exact thoughts, his emotions were as plain as their shared pain.

Scaramond closed his eyes, directing a sense of love and belonging directly to her. He tried to withhold his frustration at her jealousy.

"Are you alright," Misty asked.

"Fine," Scaramond said, curtly. "The bond chafes. Orange Skies gets fractious any time there's just a little..." he searched for a word, then gave up with a sigh. "I wish I could..." Again, he was lost for a word. He knew what he wanted to say. That the bond was too much. That he would like to break it. That his bond companion's constant pain was a burden he would gladly rid himself of. But voicing those thoughts felt like betrayal. He could no longer recall the years before the Shattering, when he and Orange Skies were inseparable friends. He could only recall the fire.

"Nobody can ever know what it is to be you," said Misty, "To know your loss. I can only say that I am here, and you may come to sit with me at any time. It doesn't betray her memory to feel comfort."

"There's the difficulty, though. If it were her only memory, my pain would be simple."

He leaned back, stroking the parchment. It felt smooth beneath his fingers, but indentations lay where the ink was slowly eating itself through the white surface. *It's time to transcribe this book once more*, he thought, astonishing himself at the length of time it had been since the last transcription. *Maybe I should scribe some of these words into stone.*

"Time gets away from me. I went down to some of my libraries the other day to find that the ink had totally dissolved the pages." He thought. "Hmm. I say the other day, but I think it may have been nearly a century ago. I had simply forgotten to put them in stasis. Do you know how long it takes for iron gall ink to completely destroy a book? It's not a fast process. I think I have forgotten more close friends than most distant acquaintances people ever meet in a lifetime. Memory fades.

Orange Skies is always with me."

Misty blinked slowly at him, then started to hum. The first notes were familiar, and Scaramond closed his eyes. He followed the tune, then he lifted his voice in time.

"Waters rushing down foreign mountains,
Glinting in light from blistering suns.
Travel through valleys
Seen by no other,
Soaring new skies beyond the mirror.

"Children of Mageunt and Draconid
Seeding the stars with our promises.
Someday our greatest
Spawning galaxies,
Birthing the Mother's new Universe."

Misty's voice stilled in time with Scaramond's.

"Thank you for singing with me. I did not know those words, but I knew the tune. I will add the words into my hoard so that I may pass it along."

"The tune is old. This was a song I learnt far before we had come to Varthien. I recall the previous planet; Prithant, I think it was called — its rocks were red with iron, but there were so many of us. We, just a few, chose to open the mirror and breed our own line in a new world. Kerathna scried the place, and said it was good, it was fresh, it was green and the metal was rich, but we came and we were not alone. And the peoples here were so much like us, some thought they must also be a Mageunt line. I never did, but some were overcome with the similarities. And then there was the greed and the fear that others would follow us, and of course the Humans wanted to protect their planet (we destroyed their economic systems, you know). I don't think anyone realised that the Shattering would cause such damage. If we could only get the pieces of the mirror all into one place..." Scaramond's voice drifted off. "But I'm prattling. You've brought an old man some joy. But I really do need to go through some of my books on display — make certain they're not in disrepair. I'll take my leave."

He rose, his face turned away from Misty as he left so she wouldn't see his tears.

Chapter 19

TITINGARN

Ford's Hold

Lance Titingarn carefully unfolded the paper. It had come in the night, bound to the leg of a tired pigeon, and Lance had collected it himself on his morning stroll to the loft. He'd been checking that the cooks were crushing the eggshell fine enough before depositing it in the feed, and the obviously underfed pigeon had rushed up to see what was on offer.

The missive was entirely unexpected. King Hrodolf of Karasta, supporting his claim to the Qoth throne? A laugh broke from his throat, setting the birds into unrest around him.

"Sorry, my doves," he said to the feathered masses around him. "I'll leave you in peace."

He all but danced down the stairs, his jubilant mood lifting him all the way to the stables for their morning inspection. Every person he saw greeted him with a smile, a nod, a "G'morning, Lord," and he responded in kind, greeting each person by name, asking after their family or pets. By the time the horses were in view, he had decided what to do about Karasta.

"Pat," he called out to one of the younger hands, "Could you run to Vashun for me and ask him to meet me in my study at, oh," he shielded his eyes, looking at how far the sun had risen and running some mental arithmetic, "about 9, I suppose? I'll be up there soon, after checking today's training."

Training was a thing he had introduced to his hold to the laughter of his peers, but which had paid off immensely. Lance had offered every able-bodied person under him arms and twenty days a year paid training to bear those arms, spaced out to a day every couple of weeks. The program had been a huge success, and people had joined up enthusiastically. Each day would be another group, and he now had full attendance throughout the week without putting a strain on anyone's work capacity.

Morale across the region had risen once people had a guaranteed income, and far from encouraging riots, as his peers had suggested, banditry had dropped significantly and arming his populace had made him more loved and respected. Lance put that down directly to trust. He trusted his people, and they trusted him. Simple.

Most days training was simple—he showed his face, checked in with a few people, checked numbers, then headed back inside for his paperwork. He'd return to the training grounds at 4pm with a bag of ceramic tokens stamped with his seal. Since instating this regime, the local economy had taken off and people were moving into his land. People were using the tokens as currency throughout his holdings, and whenever the tokens were presented to his Bursar, they would be traded for more recognisable currency, though people were starting to reject the Rin that had been the predominant currency in Qoth under the former Queen in favour of the Karastan Guilder or the Pavane Trucent.

As Lance approached the break in the tall wall that surrounded the training ground, he noticed a group of younger trainees clustered in the shadows, focussed on some sort of altercation. Quietly, he stepped up behind them to see the issue.

One boy, who looked to be around twelve, was sparring with a girl of maybe ten. His height, strength, and technique were all greater than the younger child, and she was quickly driven to the ground.

"Now you're down there," the boy proclaimed, "everything

you have is mine." He held out a hand, not to help the child up, but in expectation of payment. Jeers broke out from the surrounding crowd, telling the girl to pay up.

Lance cleared his throat loudly. "What seems to be going on here," he asked.

"I beat her, fair and square. That means everything she owns is mine now." The boy didn't appear at all perturbed at the fact an adult was asking things of him; he responded as if he were simply explaining the situation.

Lance tilted his head, considering. "And why does that mean everything she has is yours?"

"It's Right of Conquest. I conquested her, so her gear is mine."

Lance took a deep breath, his brow furrowed. He worked to keep his voice light and level. "I think you mean 'conquered', not 'conquested'. And doesn't that only apply if we're at war?"

"But we *are* at war, dummy. My dad said. Mum's really worried about it."

"Hmm. Civil war. Yes, Qoth is in a bit of turmoil right now, but the local area hasn't really been affected much. So who is this enemy of yours backing?"

"Huh? What do you mean? I just want her stuff."

"So you have no idea of her political affiliations?"

The boy scrunched his nose up. "Doesn't matter. She's rich."

"Oh." Lance straightened stiffly. "In that case, I believe banishment may be appropriate. What say you?"

The girl's eyes opened wide in fear, and the boy snickered. "Yeah, banish her."

Lance opened his eyes in mock astonishment. "Her? Oh, no, dear boy, I'm talking about you. You've committed an act of banditry in the bounds of my holdings. I'm fully within my rights to fine you, imprison you, banish you, or even execute you."

The boy backed away, confused at the change of direction.

"What? You can't do that. Lord Titingarn wouldn't let you. You're just his accountant. He just gets you to pass out his fake money."

"Oh, I'm sure Lord Titingarn would have no problems with it. But he won't banish you, not for a first offence. He will, instead, fine you 30 Rin, payable in whichever currency you have. You may choose imprisonment instead, I suppose. Additionally, you will no longer be welcome in the local militia. Any arms that have been received will need be returned."

The children in the group were nudging each other, whispering, and Lance could hear a couple of giggles.

"Do you know what you did wrong?"

"N-no" The boy had backed himself all the way to the fence, and he now had nowhere to move to.

"First, you decided that the instructions to only work on the pells except during supervised one-on-one spar time didn't apply to you. Trainees are not to fight each other.

"Second, you decided that a fight against someone smaller and weaker than you was a fair fight. It's not. However, fair doesn't matter in war. It does matter in this instance, because third, you are not at war with this girl. Well," he mused, looking over at the girl, "You weren't a war with her before today, but I suspect you may have gained an enemy.

"Fourth, you didn't apply the rules of combat before applying the rule of conquest. You can only claim conquest against a genuine enemy combatant. Otherwise, you're just indiscriminately attacking people on the road, which is banditry. Banditry is declared illegal by Lord Titingarn.

"Fifth, you didn't pay attention. I'm not just Lord Titingarn's accountant. I'm Lord Titingarn." He turned to the crowd around them. "You all need to get back to your pells. Now."

Without taking his eyes off the offender, he reached out a hand to the girl to help her up.

She took his hand and stood. "I don't need to give him any

money, do I?"

"No. Has he done this before?"

"Not to me, but I think he's done this to other girls in the group."

Lance reached out to grab the young man's wrist, who was trying to edge his way along the fence. "Then let's get to the bottom of all this. You, young man, are coming with me. After all, as Lord Titingarn's 'accountant', I need to get all the numbers in order, don't I?"

A chat to the sergeant revealed that the boy, whose name was Jak, was already on a warning. Once he'd gained all of the necessary details, he dragged the boy with him up to his study for his next appointment.

Vashun was already waiting, hands held neatly behind his back and inspecting a painting outside the study door.

"Come in, Vashun, and shut the door behind you," Lance said cheerfully, striding in and pulling out a cushioned chair from the edge of the room. "Sit, Jak, no use trying to get away. Your accounts will be dealt with as soon as I've finished with some other 'accountancy' I have in front of me."

Vashun looked at the boy with curiosity, but sat in a sofa towards the middle of the room. "Pat said you sounded like there was something urgent. Border disputes?"

"Not yet, but it's only a matter of time. Much more today than yesterday." Lance pulled out the small note from his pocket and passed it to his constable. "Karasta has tipped his hat for me. Even if I wanted to avoid the conflict, I can't anymore." He turned to Jak. "So, what are your political affiliations, boy?"

Jak stared back. "What?"

"Who would you like to rule Qoth?"

"I don't know. Does it matter?"

Lance sighed. "Yesterday I would have said that no, it didn't matter, but today it does. Never mind." He turned back to Vashun. "I need you to send envoys to our neighbours. Get them on our side. I need someone to go to Pavane. We've had some good trade with her in the past, so she may be an ally. Get smiths working on polearms, and particularly spears. We've got swords. Get shields produced — I don't want to waste metal on armour if I can help it."

Vashun carefully folded the note back up, his long brown fingers running over the creases as he thought about its contents. "Do we announce to the hold yet?"

After a moment of silence, Lance nodded. "Notify staff in the manor. Don't let them find out second-hand. I'll interrupt the training today and talk with them personally. I heed heralds across the hold calling for volunteers to the war effort. Make certain we express sadness that we will be battling our own countrymen, and double down that we must try to avoid conflict if we can win with persuasive tactics instead. No plunder — we don't plunder our own and even though we fight today, tomorrow the defeated force will be my subjects (remember that one, Jak). Let's approach this conflict with compassion."

Vashun nodded. "Anything else?"

"That should do for the moment. I'll probably think of more actions through the day, so I'll carry a tablet and jot things down as they occur to me. I'll find you if I think of something urgent."

"Thank you. I'll get those notices sent out." Lance watched as his military commander walked out, long black braid bobbing with each step.

"War's coming here?" Jak's voice was small, no trace of the bravado he showed earlier. "Does that mean we'll have to fight for real?"

"Yes, Jak. It's not quite so attractive now that it's happening, is it?"

The boy shook his head.

"Look, I don't want to imprison you, and the sergeant tells me your family isn't well-off, so here's what we'll do. You're going to work off your debt. You have today to get some basic items and let your parents know what's happening, then you can present yourself in the morning to the training sergeant. He will know you're coming. You will be assigned a cot and you will live in the manor. You will then present yourself to me, and you will accompany me throughout each day. You will carry my messages, fetch things, prepare my tea, and so on. Can you read?"

Jak shook his head.

"Time to change that. You will have reading lessons with me each evening, as I will require you to sort my correspondence. You will get to see the war. Thirty Rin works out to be roughly 6 months, so you will probably see war up close, unfortunately. You may even get to see more of the world than you ever imagined you would. Throughout this work, you will refrain from all behaviour akin to that I witnessed this morning. I cannot afford to lose any citizen unnecessarily, and that includes you, so you will receive the skills you need to survive without resorting to criminal behaviour. Does that suit?"

Jak nodded, astonished at the fairness of the offer.

"Good. Now scurry along. My day is going to be unusually busy. I will see you again tomorrow."

Chapter 20

Wamanil Clan

The sound of arguing broke through Norman's dreams of claws and waves and wind and heat.

"...Could be asleep for days! Meanwhile, we have an army stripping the forest looking for anything they can eat or smoke."

"I can't very well move on without him. He's my man. We'll have a weaker position without him..."

"One man doesn't change the course of an army."

"You know better than that. You're one man."

"A station. That's all. In the end I'm just one man, and if I fell, someone would step up to fill my shoes."

"He gives us persuasion."

"An army at the gate does that!"

Norman sighed and rolled out of the hammock.

"Anything to eat around here? I feel like I haven't had a bite in days."

Hrodolf and Farrar turned suddenly.

"You're awake! At last. We need to get back on the road."

Hrodolf's eager tone made Norman frown. "Back on the road?"

"Of course. We're bringing peace to Qoth. We need to move

on and rescue more from this terrible civil war."

Norman's frown deepened. "Is this why we had so many with us?"

"Yes." Hrodolf looked at Norman in incredulity. "We announced it at the border. Karasta is here to rescue its neighbours."

"You bring peace with a war force. That seems counterintuitive. Nevertheless, I have duties elsewhere. You'll have to rescue your neighbours without me."

Farrar snorted with barely contained laughter. "I told you. We could have moved on yesterday."

"But…" Hrodolf's head whipped between the two men, uncertain who to look at. "You're my man, Norman. You're Sharpstone. I need Sharpstone."

"My duties as Magus are more pressing at the moment. Do you need me to pay scutage?"

"I… Yes. Scutage."

Norman reached an emaciated hand into a pocket and rummaged around. He grunted. "I don't have the coin on me right now, but… hold on a tick."

He pulled his hand from his pocket and held it palm up in front of him. His eyes closed gently as he took a deep breath, and slowly a pile of golden specks gathered in the centre of his hand. As the pile grew, he cupped his other hand around it, protecting it from the wind.

"Get me a bowl, or a tight pouch, or something. I'm sure you don't want to be hauling a handful of gold dust around without something to keep it in."

Farrar's eyes were wide as he ran off, shouting to his men. "I need a bowl. And scales! I need scales!"

By the time he was back, both hands were cupped around a large pile of gold.

"About time you're back. This is getting heavy."

"How much scutage do you intend to pay?" Hrodolf asked,

looking in wonder at the rare metal.

"However much this buys me."

"If the Magus can create gold like this, doesn't that defeat the point of giving it a price?" Farrar's eyebrows were raised, half in wonder, but the other half in a cynicism born of long dealing with frauds and liars.

"I didn't create the gold. I simply collected it. We're on a beach, and the sand is filled with gold. Not much — maybe one in 50,000 grains is gold, but it's enough to make a few coins." He dusted his hands off into the glazed bowl that Farrar had provided, then turned away. Gazing towards the beach, he spotted a familiar pair on the strand, accompanied by a brown-skinned girl in a ragged blue dress.

"Is that Peter and Petunia there? How are *they* here?"

Farrar moved to the Magus's shoulder, leaving Hrodolf to his avaricious weighing of gold.

"Yes. Peter is the boy, Petunia the dragon, and the girl in blue is my daughter, Clara. I wanted to talk to you about her, actually."

"Peter and Petunia should be in Bakar, far to the North."

"They were here when we arrived. He took care of you. You may not recall. Too long awake does strange things to a man's mind. I'm not surprised you slept for two days."

Norman had pulled a sandwich from his pocket and was chewing thoughtfully.

"What is it you want to discuss?"

"Clara. His Majesty is going to lead even more chaos into the region, and she's just walked through a country in civil war, watched her entourage die in front of her, been kidnapped, and escaped from her captors only to find herself strung up by pyksees."

"Pyksees? Here? I didn't think there was a colony in this region. I'll have to check that our tracking is up to date."

"Your friends saved her. I don't know why they're here, but

I'm grateful they are."

"And you want to thank me? I did nothing."

"No. I want you to find her somewhere safe. Somewhere away from the conflict. If things get bad…"

"Ah." Norman looked at the trio on the beach and thought for a moment. "I believe Peter's involved with setting up a school in the North. Bakar, in Arac. I don't know what the board price is, but it's an option."

Together they walked over to the two teens who were playing tag with Petunia. Laughter floated on the air towards them, and Norman smiled. It was nice to see such purity after all the grief and anger he'd experienced in the past few weeks.

"Peter! Petunia!" he called out, and the trio stopped, turning to him with wide smiles.

"You're awake! It's about time. I thought you were going to sleep for the next year." Peter reached the Magus first and used a hand to steady himself against Norman's shoulder as he lifted a leg and dusted the powdery sand off his ankles and legs. "I didn't want to leave you alone, but Scaramond only gave me a week away, and it's day four now. Stuff to do."

"Thank you for waiting. It's good to see you. A pleasant surprise after such a sad time. But I'll get you to stay just a little longer. This gentleman would like to speak to you. And his daughter, too, I imagine."

Farrar straightened himself to his full height. "Yes. Clara, attend.

"The Magus has informed me that you have a school in the North. I would like Clara to attend."

"It's not set up yet, but when we're ready I can…"

"I'd like her to attend immediately. You're able to transport her, I presume?"

"What? You're sending me away?" Clara's voice was high and strained.

"You need to be far from the conflict. It's already affected you too much. It will do you good to travel, see other cultures."

"I've travelled," Clara complained. "I've walked across an entire country."

"And now you can travel to Arac and see the wonders of its inland cities. Bakar is, from all reports, a lovely place. No use getting upset; I have made my decision."

"Yes, Papa."

"I suppose we can take Clara. Petunia, are we able to cut our journey short? I'm sorry we can't…"

"We can have Clara? She's a great treasure, better than metal. Misty will love her; Clara can tell her new stories. Let's go. Let's go now!"

"We don't have board prices set up yet…"

Farrar interrupted with a deep noise in his throat. "Not a worry. Keep it fair, and I'll cover it. I'm not without funds. Invoice me when you have the prices set and you'll get paid, in ceramic, metal, or other items—whatever suits you best."

Peter looked over at Clara. "I'm sure we could find you some guest accommodation until we have the dorms set up. And you could learn how to do the things I do…"

Norman looked at Peter, frowning slightly. "Well, she may not have talent."

Petter huffed. "We just need to get her into the right environment."

"It's not about environment, or even knowledge."

"If mum can use magic by accident, Clara can do it if she sets her mind to it. It's just applying yourself, that's all." Peter turned to Clara, his eyes filled with hope and expectation. "You can become a mage, like me, and you won't be in danger, and we can spend more time together. Oh, and with Petunia, of course. Can't she, Petunia?" He looked at the tiny dragon, who seemed to barely notice that she had been an afterthought, because she was gazing at Clara with big eyes.

"Yesyesyesyes! Clara can come and play with me and we

can be great friends."

"So it's settled. You're coming to Bakar with me."

The determination on Clara's face had faded as everyone spoke at her rather than to her, and she now wore a look of resignation. She sighed. "Right. When are we going?"

Peter looked across at Norman. "Will you be coming with us?"

"I think so," Norman said. "I'd like to have a chat with Scaramond about this school, and a few other bits and pieces. We can get going as soon as you're ready."

Farrar smiled. "Thank you for this. I'll feel so much better when my little girl is safe."

"I'll grab my things." Clara turned and walked her way back up the beach.

"Say goodbye to the King for me," Norman said to Farrar. "I think he'll try to keep me here if I stick around any longer."

Chapter 21

Bakar

Peter had never considered the logistics of multiple mages teleporting extra people before. Norman had been so focussed on trying to figure out who was being transported by whom, and so Peter had just become bored and moved them to Bakar all at once. This seemed to miff Norman even worse, even though he hadn't even felt it when they'd moved, and there was suddenly a heated conversation about consent going on.

"You can't cast magic on people without consent... You can't transport people without consent... You need to let people know when you cast..."

Consent. That was rich, given what Norman had done. His mum could barely stand to touch anything magical now, she was so scared. Where was the consent then? Do as I say, not as I do? But conventions required civility, so rather than take up the argument that bit inside him, he followed lines dictated by protocol—"I offer you and your court sanctuary that you might find respite. Rest and be filled."

This brought Norman's tirade to a halt. His eye twitched as the formulaic words spilled from his mouth from between clenched teeth, "I bear good will and respect. I and my court accept your offer in peace that we rest and be filled."

Thankfully, that was where Norman's words ended. They

fell silent, an uncomfortable Clara dragging her toe across the deep carpet, watching the pile darken, then lighten as her toe swept it the other direction.

The guest floor was bare and clean, as always, with its floating orb in the centre and doors lining the walls. Peter recalled how this place had seemed so wondrous when he was a child, but he now knew the secret of the orb, how it was controlled by a series of removable tiles that linked to specific locations across the planet. One of those tiles lay flat against his chest, tied with twine he had rolled himself, covered and concealed by his tunic.

"Mountain?" he asked Norman, expecting the usual.

"Shard Sea, I think," Norman replied. Peter looked the mage in surprise. In the entire time he had known Norman, he had never chosen another view. However, he chose not to speak, setting the room choice to view the Shard Sea.

"What about you, Clara? Is there anywhere special you'd like to look out on in your room? I can set your balcony to view deserts, oceans, ice scapes, mountains, beaches..."

"Can it just show me this place? Where I am?" Clara's voice was soft, almost pleading.

Peter had never considered the idea of not wanting to look at somewhere else. Wouldn't you want to look at other parts of the world, see new sights? "Um, yes, I suppose so. But don't you want somewhere exciting?"

"This is really exciting, being here. I was on a beach just a moment ago. Now I'm in a room with no windows and lots of doors, and a big thing floating in mid-air." She hugged herself, brushing sand off her arm, then realised it was falling onto the carpet. "Sorry, I can clean that up..."

"No need," Peter said. "The room cleans itself. Scaramond doesn't like what he calls 'petty distractions' so he set it all up to be self-cleaning."

Clara's eyes opened wide at that. Peter remembered the way he had reacted when he'd first learned that he didn't need to try sweeping the carpet. His first reaction had been wonder, and his second had been despair at the thought that he wouldn't have anything to do.

"There will be plenty of things to keep you occupied without worrying about this room," he reassured her, then showed her to her door. "Petunia, can you show Clara how everything works? I'm going to find Scaramond and let him know we're back."

Bounding up the moving stairs two at a time, Peter met only disappointment when he found Scaramond's chamber empty. Puffing, he looked back at the stairs, then decided he didn't want to take such a slow way down. Grinning to himself, he *stepped* to another place.

One moment he was on the ninth floor, and the next he was striding onto the gravel outside the tower. At least, that was his intention. He frowned. This didn't look like Scaramond's gardens. The gate looked similar, the path was the same coloured gravel, but the lawn? He turned, taking in the stone buildings that rose all around him. Then he stopped. Scaramond's tower rose there, behind him. He was in the right place, but in four days there must have been thousands of people building to get to this stage of completion.

He spotted Chance wandering out of one of the buildings and waved. "Hey, Chance," he called, "Where did all of this come from? I'm looking for Scaramond, but I think I'll get lost if I move."

Chance walked over, a wry smile on his face, and motioned with his head in a way that said "Follow me." So, that's exactly what Peter did, happily chattering his one-sided story to his silent friend, telling him tales of pyksees and exploding Pojeru fruit and Chirren and new companions. By the time they reached Misty's cave, Peter was detailing the armour and weapons of the Karastan army, wielding an imaginary sword to show the strike techniques he had learned from soldiers, Chance nodding along with interest.

The cave had changed, too. Curtains now swathed the walls, and rugs covered the floor, making the place look less like a hole in the ground and more like a home. Movement from a circular cushion—a mattress almost—in the centre of the room focussed Peter's gaze on Misty, whose sides were starting to grow tiny filaments which would eventually become new wings, fed by the neat piles of metals and ores neatly stacked to one side of the room. She lifted her head from the book before her.

"The youngling returns, Scarred One," she intoned, and a scraping sound on the stone floor sounded from behind one of the many curtains. The cloth was drawn back, and Scaramond stepped out. For just a moment, Peter noted a writing desk before the curtain fell behind the red-robed mage.

"You're early," the mage said.

Peter smiled. "Yes! There's been so much that happened while I was away, and I met Chirren, and there were pyksees, and we've got our first student, and Norman's waiting for you."

"You're starting to sound like Petunia," Scaramond said with a frown on his face. "First things first, you said that the Magus is here? I didn't feel his arrival."

"In the guest quarters. I teleported them straight in."

Scaramond sighed, rubbing his forehead. "You teleported them straight in. Of course you did. A note for the future—don't do that. I get alerted if someone comes to the drive. But what if your guest had hostile intent, and you let them straight in without having to navigate security?"

"It's just Norman," Peter blurted out. "He's harmless."

"Stop." Scaramond's face filled with thunder. "Do not ever call him harmless. That is no longer 'just Norman'. That's the Magus. You may feel you know him, but he is now the most politically powerful creature on this planet. Respect power. He is no longer to be regarded as a trusted friend and you must never underestimate him. He may be an ally today, but alliances can shift."

Scaramond strode from the room, an apologetic Chance

following close at his heels, leaving a bewildered Peter to look at Misty. "What was that?" he asked. "Did something bad happen?"

Misty chuckled wryly. "It's not you. He's just had some reminders of a harsher time come up while you were away. He's right though. No matter how you feel about Norman, he's not harmless, and you should keep that in mind."

Chapter 22

Bakar

The room was almost as large as the entire house she had been trapped in just a few days before. Soft carpet, canopied bed, dressers and cupboards with fine marquetry—it was like Clara had been transported from the depths of squalor into the most luxuriant palace in just an instant. She looked down at her tattered blue shift, picking at it with a grubby hand, and a confused feeling bubbled up from her gut and choked her throat. Tears inexplicably filled her eyes and a long wail escaped her mouth.

Petunia fluttered anxiously to the girl. "It's okay. Peter's mum can fix your dress. She's good at that."

"No," Clara wailed, "I don't care about my dress, I just... I don't know. I don't know what's wrong." Great, heaving sobs shook her. "I left home with my nanny and five guards to go to my father, and they died, and I got to the border by myself, and I was taken, and I escaped, but I was lost, and there were pyksees, and then you and then the Chirren, and then I found my father but he sent me away and now I'm here and it's... it's just big."

"Oh." Petunia's voice was small. "Well, how about I show you the bathroom? You could have a nice bath and get clean, and that might help you feel a bit better."

Clara followed the little dragon into the adjoining room,

which was smaller than the room she had just been in but not by much. The bathtub was carved from a single piece of smoky quartz, the tiny inclusions sparkling in the diffuse light. The artist had carved a seascape all around the sides of the tub, and Clara could almost hear the crashing of the waves as she looked at it.

"The buttons put water in the bath," Petunia was saying, and Clara forced her mind away from the art. "The red one is hot and the blue one is cold, so you can make it just right. I like it when it's hot. And you can put bubbles in. The bubbles are like soap, but they aren't soap, and they smell nice."

The little dragon was pressing buttons as she spoke, and suddenly white, frothy bubbles were tumbling into the water. A delicate scent of roses and jasmine filled the air.

"Well, what are you waiting for? When you're finished, get out and touch the white button and you'll get all dry again."

Clara looked towards the white button, then she looked at a nearby seat with a hollow in the centre. Another button sat next to it. "What's that yellow button for?"

Petunia stuck out her bottom lip in thought, then shrugged. "Dunno. Human things, I suppose. I'll leave you alone to get undressed. Maybe I can find you something to wear."

The dragon flapped her way out, and Clara quickly lifted her dress off and dipped a foot in, immediately lifting it back out when she realised that when Petunia said 'hot', she meant very hot. She tapped the blue button and felt for the temperature. When it reached a more human temperature, Clara stepped back in.

The heat melted into Clara's bones, relaxing all of her muscles. A soft cloth from the side of the tub lifted off the dirt that had worked its way into the very pores of her skin. She scrubbed her fingers through her hair, teasing out the knots as her curls relaxed in the water. Finally, feeling clean for the first time in weeks, Clara stepped from the water onto the mat sitting beside the bath.

The white button blasted her with warm air and suddenly

she was dry and staring at her reflection in the mirror. She almost didn't recognise herself. Her hair, once a deep chestnut brown, was now almost blonde from the sun. Her skin, already dark, had further darkened to a deep, golden brown hue, with a smattering of darker freckles across her nose. When she had left her mother's house, she had been plump, and now she was thin, muscled, wiry. She glanced at the heap of dirty blue fabric on the floor, then bent to pick it up, wondering if she could wash it then use that white button to dry it again.

"I've found something," Petunia's distant voice sounded from behind the door. "I'll put it on the bed for you."

Relief flooded Clara, and she dropped the dress again. It hadn't felt comfortable for some time, and the image in the mirror had shown her why.

The dress Petunia had laid out for Clara was different to anything she'd ever seen before. It was bulkier, layered, covering a great deal more of her skin than Qoth fashion normally dictated. But it was pretty, green and yellow with little embroidered flowers on the apron and frills at the neck. Dressed in the heavy cloth that felt like a warm hug, she turned to the balcony for the first time and stepped out.

Immediately she realised why the clothing was so much bulkier. Even through the layers, the wind chilled her, even though the sun shone down upon her. She absently scratched at the back of her arm, feeling itchy from the heavier fabric.

Looking out across Bakar, she saw rooftops stretching before her. In the distance, there were mountains topped with white. She could see that the estate the tower sat upon was large, and its buildings were a different construction to those outside its bounds, and that there were areas of the estate that were wooded, deep green instead of the bright and glossy tones of the jungle. Somewhere to her left she could make out the bright sounds of a smith beating the 'ting, ting' of metal on metal, the sound drifting on the air alongside the rich, foreign smells of foods she had never encountered before. A buzz of excitement filled her. Trepidation at the unfamiliar, yes, but also a sense that this was an adventure.

She stepped away from the balcony and turned to the door, ready to make her way into the city she had just seen.

Chapter 23

Finery

Bakar

Scaramond noticed his pace was hurried and forced himself to slow down. He steadied his breathing, slowing the in-out in time with the ancient focus mantra that he had learnt as a child. He felt Orange Clouds rolling in distress, banging herself against the soft-hard walls of her molten tomb, and he willed the mantra to her, hoping she might feel its rhythms and be calmed.

Footsteps now stately, back unbowed, face impassive, he walked through the doors to his tower and onto the stairway. He allowed it to lift him, taking every second to consider the conversations he would have with the fresh Magus.

It was encouraging that Norman had chosen to visit so early in his tenure, Scaramond considered. Some left it months, even years, into their seat before reaching out. Of course, others never reached out and Scaramond had to go to them—those leaders were not ideal. Feeling his pulse becoming more rapid at memories of harsher times, Scaramond once more wrested his thoughts back to the present.

Norman. How had he found Peter again, so far from Arac? That was an interesting coincidence, particularly after the lengths he had gone to to remove the boy from Norman's direct influence. Whether it was a good coincidence or a bad one, time would tell, and if there's something Scaramond had a lot of, it was time.

Reaching the fifth floor, he stepped from the stairway, coming face to face with the Magus. Norman's stature had changed in the few weeks since he had last seen him. He stood taller, straighter. His face, too, had changed. There were new lines, or deeper lines perhaps, making Norman look more mature, angrier, sadder.

With a deliberately welcoming smile, Scaramond bowed low. "Greetings, Magus. I trust that Peter has offered you traditional welcome to the grounds?"

Norman cocked an eyebrow but didn't return the smile. *Interesting*, Scaramond thought.

"Yes. Peter has been an excellent host so far. My apologies for not announcing myself ahead of time, but fate seems to have afforded me a window. I was hoping to take a look at this school that you and Peter are proposing, and I've brought you your first boarder. Her father is prepared to pay boarding fees so long as they're fair. Peter has set her up in the room across from mine."

Scaramond glanced across, and indeed, two of the room chevrons were lit on opposite sides of the room.

"Well, if it's a tour, we may as well all go together." He stepped across to the indicated door and knocked.

Almost immediately, Petunia was opening the door, using the special "Petunia-height" latches that Scaramond had installed specifically for her.

"Clara's taking a bath," she announced in a solemn stage-whisper. "She's sad right now. She needs clothes. Good ones that are clean and not torn. That will make her happy. Then she won't cry. Can I have some clothes for Clara?"

Norman frowned. "I don't think it's clothing that's making her sad, but it's a reasonable ask." He pulled from elsewhere and a gown appeared, draped over his arm.

Scaramond looked at the fabric. It certainly wasn't the most expensive dress, but the embellishments marked this an upper-end garment. "Very nice quality. I'm sure the girl will get some good wear out of it. You have such garments easily to hand?"

Norman frowned again. "What does it matter where it came from? It will fit the child, and she needed it." He handed it to Petunia, and she flapped her way slowly inside, looking overburdened. Scaramond filed the information mentally.

The dragon's voice drifted out from the bedroom, "I've found something. I'll put it on the bed for you." She then flew back to the two, pulling the door closed behind her. "Clara will be out soon, I'm sure. I showed her how to use all the buttons. Except for the yellow one. I have no idea what that does."

"So, how have the first weeks as Magus been treating you? I imagine you're spending a lot of time fielding invitations from various countries. Always happens."

Norman turned to him. "Yes. I've been a few places so far. Actually, it was my trip to Karasta that placed Peter into my path."

Scaramond kept his face impassive. "Oh? Of course, he was heading to that part of the world. A personal errand, I believe. Although he was nowhere near Lanrash. How did you encounter him?"

"I wasn't going to Lanrash, actually. Not at first. I decided to group my visits by geographical proximity, so Wamanil first, to speak with the Chirren, then Sharpstone. My... mother decided to invite the Karastan nobility to be reintroduced to me."

Scaramond's eyebrows shot up. "Your mother? I had no idea..."

"Yes. It gave me a chance to get instated as Earl Sharpstone at the same time as being introduced."

"You were entitled? Albert didn't tell me."

"Albert probably didn't know. I wasn't exactly first in line when he took me as apprentice."

"I don't think we've ever had a Magus that held mundane title too," Scaramond mused. His mind whirled at the ways this could complicate politics.

"Yes. I look forward to exploring the precedent. Which reminds me, I'll need assistance. Are you familiar with the workings of the succession box? You taught Albert, after all…"

"Yes, I can walk you through its use…"

Scaramond's thought process was interrupted by the door beside them opening.

"Clara! You look so pretty," Petunia gushed. "Green looks nice on you. Blue looks nice too, but green is what you're wearing now and it's nice. And your hair looks pretty too. It's all fluffy. Not like before when you were still dirty."

Taking advantage of Norman's shift in attention, Scaramond glanced at the slip of a girl before him, training all his detection ability on her. There was nothing. Not even a glimmer of Mageunt heritage. She was pure Varthien stock—a relative rarity. Most held a tiny amount of the ability the Mageunt had bred into the population, but this child was wholly indigenous to the planet.

She would be useless.

Chapter 24

Bakar

Peter had dawdled on his way back, using the time to build a map of the area in his mind. How he would ever find his way through the mass of buildings, he didn't know, but at least he could remember this one path. Every time he felt he might be moving in the wrong direction he sought out the tall tower on the horizon and oriented himself toward it. The silent buildings looked down upon him eerily; he couldn't imagine there could be so many magical children in the entire world to fill them.

Eventually he reached the tower and stepped onto the bottom stair to take him up. The staircase lifted him steadily past the first two floors of the library, then between the greenhouse and the dining hall he encountered everyone else coming down.

This always looked somewhat strange. His eyes would try to move to other things rather than look at the place where up and down superimposed over each other, and focussing on the place where the two directions met would grey out his vision. Today, however, his vision drew itself to Clara, who was clean, smiling, dressed in a beautiful green gown. Dark freckles danced over her face, and her hair sparkled as if caught in sunlight. She looked at him, and her eyes were large and brown, like gleaming agates.

He wanted her to look at him and smile all the time, he

decided. He smiled back. With a thought, the stairs he travelled on reversed direction, and he started moving back down with the rest of the group.

"Ah, here is my young colleague now." Scaramond's voice cut through the layers of Clara in Peter's head, and he reluctantly looked away from her. "You have something for me, I believe?"

"Oh! The fruit!" Peter fumbled in his pocket for the small bag. "It was a challenge getting the stasis spell right. The fruit kept exploding and juicing themselves. But I managed to get you ten."

Scaramond took the bag, opened it, and removed a berry. He carefully peeled back the green hood, then popped the exposed berry into his mouth. His eyes drifted closed, a serene expression crossing his face. "Oh yes. Perfection. These are delicious, Magus; have you ever tried Pojeru?" He held the bag open towards Norman, who took a fruit out and pushed the entire hood to his lips.

Sucking the juice through the gaps in the hood, Norman nodded, then pulled the green remnants away. Blue-black juice stained his lips. "I grew up in Karasta, where Pojeru grows wild. The trick is to eat the fruit while it's still on the vine. Picking it tends to ruin the fruit. Thank you for this taste of my childhood; it's a good memory from a difficult time."

Peter stared in disbelief. "You asked me to get these because you just want to *eat* them? I thought they were going to be some rare spell ingredient! I was in danger! I could have been killed."

Scaramond waved a hand nonchalantly at him as he stepped off the stairs on the ground floor. "You weren't in danger. You're a mage. There's nothing in that area of the world that can meet your level of ability."

"There were pyksees!"

Scaramond's eyebrows lifted. "Pyksees. My goodness. And how did you deal with that?" His voice was dry, not a trace of concern anywhere in his face.

"I set them on fire," Petunia announced proudly. "And they

went 'Squeeeee' and crumpled up like spiders and fell out of the sky and then we found Clara and we ran away."

"See? No danger. Petunia was able to take care of them, and she's a child." Scaramond's voice was light, but Norman's face darkened. "If you'd had your mind about you, you could have avoided the colony entirely."

"If we'd avoided the colony, Clara would be dead." Peter stared at the man flatly.

"Hm, yes. Clara." Scaramond's attention focussed on the teenaged girl. "What are we to do with you?" He led the group outside to the drive.

"We teach her how to use her magic," Peter said. "That's what the school is for."

Scaramond looked at Peter in surprise. "Magic? I'm afraid that's impossible. Clara has no magical talent. We can certainly offer her scholarship…"

"What do you mean, Clara has no magic? How do you know?"

Scaramond turned his attention to Clara. "Girl, have you ever displayed any magical ability?"

Clara's eyes were large. "No. I don't think so."

"Have your parents got any magical talent?"

"No."

"Have you ever heard of anyone in your family being a mage?"

"Um… my second-cousin married a girl who could make plants grow faster."

"That's it?"

Clara nodded, looking scared. "What does that mean?"

Scaramond turned back to Peter. "Magical talent runs in families. There are certain markers that point to magic — the chin, the earlobes, the cheekbones, the eye shape — but a better indicator is to look directly for the spark. I suppose different mages see it differently, and as you're just coming into discovering all of that you may not have explored your vision yet, but for me it's a glimmer that increases in brightness the more power a mage commands. Clara has no glimmer. No spark. She's not a mage. Completely ordinary."

Clara looked down, embarrassed. "Sorry," she whispered.

Peter felt an anger raging red-hot through his chest. "She's not ordinary," he growled. "Clara is special. She'll show you. Just you see."

"Oh, there's nothing wrong with being ordinary," Scaramond said. "We'll find something to teach you, child, don't worry. I'm sure we have things you'll find of interest. Now, let's start by looking at the dorms..."

Chapter 25

Bakar

Scaramond led them from building to building, talking about things that Clara found utterly uninteresting, but she remained attentive the entire way, nodding, agreeing, giggling at things that were slightly funny. Sometimes Peter would ask a question, sometimes Norman, and Petunia would interject her special brand of nonsense, but Clara barely noticed when this happened. She thought back to when Scaramond said she was ordinary, then had said there was nothing wrong with being ordinary. A strange clash of emotions hit her — shame at not being the extraordinary person her parents, her nanny, and her governesses had all told her she was, but a burning warmth at the look Scaramond had given her when he had said there was nothing wrong with that.

Her eyes rested on the tall mage. He must only be a couple of years older than Peter, she thought, and he was so handsome. The floor-length red robes emphasised his height. Every time his hands moved, she was struck by how beautiful his fingers were — long and elegant like a musician. She wondered how she could draw his attention more.

She was a little puzzled by some of the rooms they entered. Classrooms had large slabs of dark slate hung upon the wall, and many of them still had writing in white chalk. However, the writing was unlike any Clara had seen before. Some figures appeared similar to the alphabet she knew, but others were so foreign that Clara couldn't begin to decipher them.

"I'm sorry to interrupt," she said just as Scaramond was explaining that, given enough staff, the school could house up to 5000 students. "But what is the writing on the walls? Will I be expected to read that?"

Scaramond looked up briefly at the work. "The writing is in Ancient Yurdelt. You won't be expected to learn it. It's a precursor language to the one we're speaking today, so some of the letter forms have been preserved down the centuries.

"This lesson appears to have been about the myths of Varthien. It's important to study the myths of cultures across the planet, as many of them have their roots in real events, and they usually have lessons that are important to acknowledge."

He turned his gaze upon her, and she felt her face start to burn. The urge to look away, look down, filled her, but she held his gaze, feeling her breath speeding up.

"This class was designed for students whose talents had yet to emerge, and those headed for politically important stations. Do you like stories? This could be a satisfactory class for you to take on."

"Yes," she breathed. "I like to read stories. I have lots of books at home."

"Good!" A large smile appeared on his face. "You've seen the library on the tower's lower floors, but that's just the most regularly accessed volumes. I've got several more libraries stashed through the grounds..." His face fell for a moment. "They'll all be written in Ancient Yurdelt. I'll have to do something about that." He grinned again. "But in the meantime, I'm sure you'll find the books in the tower more than sufficient, and Misty will enjoy telling you some of her stories."

Looking at the dorms was depressing. Long rooms filled with beds, each with a small trunk at the end, gave little privacy.

Further on, the dorms became cubicles that slept four to a cell, with study desks and tall cupboards for the inhabitants to use. Then they moved on to better accommodations — one bed per cubicle, a desk, a cupboard, and a chest of drawers. The cubicles were still open to a central hall, however.

"These dorms are all sorted by age," Scaramond was saying. "The youngest children sleep together, with supervision to avoid bullying. As they get older — nine to twelve years old - we allow them to choose who they will bunk with. Students aged thirteen to fifteen get their own cubicle."

Clara hugged herself, scratching absently at the back of her arm. "I'm fifteen, but my birthday is in a month. Where will I sleep then?"

"Aha! I'm just about to take you all to see our seniors' facilities. Students between sixteen and twenty are treated as adults. This is a little bit of a walk, so I'll teleport us all, if everyone is in agreement?"

There were nods all around, and suddenly Clara found herself outside once more, standing in front of a low building with two doors.

"Each of these buildings is a twin-apartment. The southern portions of the estate are exclusively accommodation for staff and senior students. Each apartment is self-sufficient, with a lounge, study, kitchen with dining table, bedroom, and bathroom. Seniors are still welcome to eat in the dining halls, and encouraged to mentor the younger students, but they have less regimented schedules. Clara, as your birthday is so close, we can move you into one of these apartments immediately. Shall we take a look inside?"

There were three stone steps up to the entrance, and a palm's weight was all it required to open the solid door. Stepping through the threshold, Clara looked back at the hinges, concerned that the silent opening meant leather strapping to hold the door in place. Her father had always eschewed leather strapped doors, telling her that the only thing stopping a thief was the sharpness of his blade. She was surprised to find a perfectly carved and polished hinge of wood, with a thick hinge pin of a different coloured wood.

"How does the door open so silently? The hinge should creak."

Scaramond turned to her. "The wood for these doors comes from trees that once grew in a land that doesn't exist anymore, north of the land we now call Marthune; the trees are extinct. The wood is as strong as steel and can be polished to an atomic smoothness."

"I don't know that word — atomic. What does it mean?"

Scaramond's eyes narrowed as he thought on the question. "It's rather a complex idea; not something I can easily explain. I can give you a book that will teach you the basics. For now, consider that atomic smoothness is so smooth that the finest silk is like sandpaper in comparison."

Clara nodded and filed the information away for later. She turned her attention to the room they were in. A green cushioned settee and two matching chairs sat in the middle of the room. Cabinets lined the walls, many with panels of glass in their doors.

"Glass in cabinet doors?" Clara was shocked at the overt display of wealth. "Is this the wrong apartment?"

Scaramond smiled. "Not at all. Many things are possible for the mage community that aren't easy to do when relying on artisans. In the early days we had to set down specific rules about what mages could and couldn't do regarding sale of products to humans. We almost destroyed the planetary economy. Assume nothing at the school has an artisanal origin. Except, maybe, that dress you're wearing, or a few other small nicknacks here and there."

Clara could see a small study through a doorway, the desk facing the door. Empty bookshelves flanked it either side.

"You may store any books from the library in your personal bookshelves. It would be appreciated if you make them available to other students on request, and once you've done with any avenue of study, to return them to the main repository."

Scaramond motioned her to the next door along. "Your bedroom is next to the study. It has a bathroom attached…"

Clara opened the door to the bedroom. A large bed took up most of the room, with a heavy trunk at its foot and a matching dresser and tallboy against the wall.

"You don't hang nets?" Clara hugged herself, feeling unsafe at the idea of sleeping in such a large room with no protection.

"Not generally," Scaramond said. "There's no need. We're too far North for the biting insects you're used to. However, if it feels too exposed for you," he waved a hand and the bed changed to one with a canopy, "We have others I can swap out for you. This will also trap heat for you in the middle of winter."

Clara smiled in happiness. "Thank you," she said, feeling the words deeply. She opened the door to the bathroom and found a setup almost identical to that in the guest quarters. "Oh, there's that yellow button that Petunia couldn't explain."

"Ah. Ablutions. There is no nightsoil collection. The yellow button will remove all waste from inside the privvy seat."

"Oh," Clara said, feeling silly. Of course that's what the button was for, she thought. She backed out of the bathroom and headed for the last door.

It opened onto a kitchen. Here there was an unfamiliar sight. A large, white, waist-high box with several doors in the front stood against the back wall. A round pipe led from the top of the box to the ceiling. Either side were cabinets, with a large sink to one side and a table with chairs under a curtained window to the other side.

Clara looked at the strange knobs adorning the face of the box. They seemed too loose for decorations—almost like she could twist them off.

"What's this thing? It looks very strange for a cupboard."

Scaramond chuckled. "Yes, I suppose it does look strange. It's a combustion stove cast all in ceramic. The dark sections on the top can be used for pots and pans. This door on the left is an oven, the top door to the right is a grill, and the bottom door to the right is the furnace. Fill it with wood or coal and light it up in the mornings. The buttons open and close vents to allow more or less air to various areas of the oven so you can alter the heat."

"Oh. I don't actually know how to cook. We had servants at home to do that for us."

Scaramond raised an eyebrow. "You need to know how to cook. Feeding yourself is the most important thing anyone can know. I'll set up lessons for you alongside our other student."

Norman interrupted. "I thought Clara was your first student. Peter said you weren't open yet."

Scaramond turned to the Magus. "Peter didn't know. When the buildings last went into stasis, it seems someone was still inside. Yslt is currently boarding with Felicity Diefen to acclimatise to the change."

Norman frowned in alarm. "How did the missing child not get noticed in the first place? And how long ago was she trapped?"

"The school shut down under the orders of Argentus Barduce. At the time we were housing many orphans from the Interregnum War; Yslt was one of those orphans."

Norman swallowed, his face suddenly pale. "I see. That's quite a change. I'm sure that Felicity... Felicity? Are you sure that's the best choice?"

"What's wrong with mum?" Peter objected. "My mum's a great mum."

"Mrs Diefen was grateful for the coin. She also seemed very interested in the school uniform. Which reminds me," Scaramond turned to Clara. He put out an arm and a pile of clothing appeared draped over it. "You may prefer to dress in school colours, especially once our enrollments start. We have a good stock of uniforms, so you never need to worry about clothing. Peter, I'll get you to take Clara to see your mother. Perhaps she can mend Clara's dress. You can all meet Yslt at the same time."

He carried the clothing into the bedroom, laying them on

the bed, then drew a small pouch out of his pocket.

"You may take residence immediately. Here's an allowance for you to purchase anything you need."

Clara opened the small pouch. "These coins are metal," she whispered.

"Yes. Well, no, but yes. They're ceramic with a metal coating. The country is rich, but not that rich. Otherwise people would be melting down the coin. Bit of a waste, I think, but the Arac senate likes them."

Peter had a puzzled look on his face. "But the coin I gave Petunia…"

"Silver dipped. Enough for a wyrmling. Nobody can afford to use real metal for coins anymore."

Norman's eyebrows shot up. "I never knew all our currency was ceramic. No wonder everybody loved getting change from me. I only ever paid in replicated currency, so it was metal through and through."

Scaramond tsked at him. "You'll give mages a bad name if you start forging currency, even if you're paying more than you should be. Governments like the illusion of controlling their markets."

"I have some metal," Clara announced. "I can make payments for my tutelage up front." She pulled the shackles from her pocket. "They used these on me when I was kidnapped, and I was able to use a blade to open the lock."

Norman looked at her in shock. "You were shackled? Oh, you poor child. I will make certain that your captors pay dearly for what they did."

Scaramond waved the shackles away. "I honestly have no need of your… things. Keep them, sell them. You could make a good deal of money from that much iron. But perhaps get Misty to melt them down for you first. Those things may cause questions.

"We'll be retiring for tea in the tower. Would you like to stay and get acquainted with your new home, or will you be joining us?"

Chapter 26

Bakar

The whispering was all around, in a voice that was almost words but not quite. Clara felt warm and cocooned in the golden glow, but anxious that she couldn't tell what the voices meant. She strained to hear what they were saying.

Slowly, individual voices started to emerge, but one played above all others, and Clara fixed her mind on it, listening to its cadence and tone. Its rhythms rocked her like music, like the beat of her own heart, until it was the only voice she could hear. When words appeared in her mind, she wondered if it was just her own fantasy.

"we are. be us. carry us."

The voice remained a whisper, unintelligible. But the words inside her mind echoed, overlapped, until they were louder than the outside noise.

"carry us. speak our voice. be us."

Clara's questions welled inside her, but her mouth felt stopped with a cottony substance. Instead of speech, she found herself solidifying her ideas into a point, focussing on a single thought. "Who are you?"

"we are. voice. inside. we are inside. we are Queen. be us."

"You are Queen?"

"we are Queen. we are together. we are inside. be voice."

Clara rolled over and found herself caught in the blankets on her large bed. Somehow she had wrapped her face in the sheets. It felt strange to be on the wide softness, so different from the feel of the bare ground she had slept on for weeks.

The whispers from the dream echoed in her head. She looked around, seeking familiar items to draw her further to wakefulness, but the room was dark. Muzzily, she recalled that there were blackout curtains across one wall. She felt her way across, then drew the curtains open.

A wide, glazed window filled much of the wall, and Clara gasped at the extravagance that she hadn't noticed yesterday. Her bedroom looked out over a large expanse of lawn which was backed by a dark forest that was barely visible in the early morning fog.

She reached out a hand and touched the glass. It was cold, bringing her clearly into the present. She considered the contents of the dream, clear in her mind, not fading like other dreams were wont to do.

It was a replay of her time with the pyksees, only this time divorced from the terror, and with the addition of a new voice. She felt, instead, warm and comforted inside the yellow glow. What could it mean?

She brushed aside the thoughts of the dream, then turned to consider the morning ahead of her. Yesterday's afternoon had been cakes, and then a visit to the older dragon, who seemed a little aloof, Clara thought, but had been happy to melt down the shackles for her, even suggesting that they be melted into several smaller pieces so that Clara could sell them a little at a time. A strange, sallow boy had been there. He had looked at her with a dark, brooding gaze but hadn't said a word. Clara hoped she wouldn't see a lot of him. He seemed intense.

Clara looked over at the pile of navy fabric sitting folded on the dresser. The idea of pants disgusted her. What did

Scaramond think, that she was a boy? Today, she intended to visit Peter's mother, she decided. The shift she was wearing, which was actually the innermost layer from the clothes Norman had given her yesterday, was nice, but she needed more than one outfit. She would rather not have to rewash her clothing every day.

Her tattered blue silks, so cherished by her when she had lived with her mother, had been washed and dried last night, and she wondered if Felicity could do anything to rescue them. Sadly, she considered, they may be past using. But perhaps the scraps could be repurposed, and she hoped that the expensive fabric might lessen the cost of other purchases.

She scratched at an itchy spot on the back of her arm, and stopped moving. There was a lump. Not a large lump, but something different to normal. She felt around the edges; it was longer than it was wide, and hard, and felt like it was just under the skin. She rushed to the dresser, seeking out the mirror, then angled herself so she could see the back of her arm. There was a slight redness where she had been scratching, but nothing else.

Maybe it's just a bug-bite, Clara thought. *Maybe it's nothing.* She pushed the thought to the back of her mind and focussed on more pressing things. Today she would be wearing the green and yellow dress again, and seeking out new attire.

Chapter 27

Bakar

Norman sat before Scaramond's desk.

"How about you show me what this thing can do," he said, and put a hand into his pocket.

He groped about on the table in his study, kilometres away.

"Interesting bilocation you use there," Scaramond said. "Do you ever wonder that the dimensional field will collapse? You could sever your hand and barely notice."

Norman grabbed the succession box and pulled it from his pocket.

"It's never been an issue. I didn't even think of it collapsing. Have you seen many such incidents?" He placed the box on the wide desk between them.

"One or two," Scaramond admitted, "Though, in those cases, a loss of a hand would have been the nicest outcome possible. There's a bit more disruption to the local environment. Shockwaves, earthquakes, and the like. Your hand will be fine. If the dimensional field collapses, you probably won't survive, so it's not going to matter to you long term. Just avoid fraying around the pocket and you'll be okay. Maybe reinforce it a little with something stronger than linen."

Norman nodded, his heartbeat pounding in his ears. It

wasn't so much the thought of death that alarmed him, but injuring more people around him. "Sure. Now, about this box." He lifted the lid to show an empty interior.

"Ah. Press your palm against the floor of the box."

Norman did as he was told and felt a click. An inner compartment opened and a book was revealed. He pulled it out.

"That's the Magus Journal. Every Magus has placed his thoughts and reasoning on major decisions into it down the line. You'll need to read it."

Norman put it to one side. "How about the box's instructions?"

"Repeat that press. It should open the next space."

Once more, Norman pressed his palm to the floor of the box, and a flap in the lid of the box opened up. Out fell a yellowing roll of papyrus. Noticing a dark splotch on the inside of the compartment, Norman leaned in to see. A familiar sigil was bound inside a circle.

"I've seen that mark before. It's on the pact coins, isn't it?"

Scaramond motioned to the roll. "What does it say?"

Norman picked up the roll and unfurled it. The papyrus crackled and was slightly translucent as it ran through his fingers, and he needed to hold it down to prevent it curling back up immediately.

"It's not a current language, as far as I can tell. Hold on, I have a translate I can cast that might work on written text."

He closed his eyes and concentrated, then opened them again. The letters swam a little before his eyes, but he started to comprehend pieces.

"This first one: 'The candidate must be completely loyal to Argentus Barduce.' Why is that even a consideration?"

"If that's in there, it's the original instruction. Argentus commissioned the box to deal with the issues that arose during the Interregnum War. He needed to make certain the line was stable, at least for a few years."

"Nobody ever thought to change it? That was five thousand years ago!" He stared at the crumbling papyrus in astonishment.

"You're Magus. The title doesn't change hands very often. There have only been six individuals in a position to find this text."

Norman thought about that. He read down the list further.

The candidate must set aside ethical considerations in favour of those determined by Argentus Barduce.

The candidate must not hold ambition to rise above their station.

The candidate must be content to maintain the status quo...

Norman read through the list with a growing sense of concern. More than seventy instructions, each determining that Highmage positions were filled with venal, cowardly, lazy men who were never going to rise up or cause any change to the system.

"I always thought the Council was choosing the best of us. Instead, we get what? Pompous jackasses who care more about their own luxury than on making the world better. We're mages. We can fix things. We can remove hunger and war. I need a pen. Ink. Paper. Now."

Instantly, his needs were filled, pulled from his desk in his far-away tower. He dipped the pen and started scribbling new instructions with barely a thought, heedless of the big drops of ink that fell.

The candidate must be a free thinker.

The candidate must be ethically inclined.

The candidate must be willing to put the needs of the populace above his own needs.

The candidate must seek to improve the lives of all peoples of Varthien...

On and on, he wrote, barely noticing the mage across from him who was reading each line with interest. Eventually, he slowed, blowing lightly on the paper to dry the ink.

"Do you think you've managed to capture everything

now?"

Scaramond's question snapped Norman out of his introspection.

"Oh. Yes, I suppose. I'll have time to revise later, but this is good for the moment, I think." He packed the old list away in a pocket and then fastened the new list into its previous hiding space. "How do I make announcements to the world with this thing?"

Scaramond pointed out a small panel on the side of the box. "Press that panel in and speak. Every intelligent creature will hear your words, conveniently translated into their language of choice."

Norman pressed the button and spoke.

"This is Magus Norman Linter, addressing the communities of Varthien. I declare that it is now illegal to kill other intelligent creatures for the purpose of eating them. This includes humans, chirren, and alver. It is illegal to consume the meat of an intelligent creature, except for funerary purposes as determined by the direct community of the deceased.

"I declare that pyksees are a danger to the wider population. All known pyksee colonies must be eradicated.

"I declare that any individual involved in kidnap for the purpose of ransom is to be publicly executed.

"That is all." He released the button.

"Bold start to your tenure. I am excited to see what happens," Scaramond said with a smile.

Norman started to respond, but a pressure on the back of his collar *yanked* him…

Chapter 28

Bakar

Peter beamed as he walked across the bridge with Clara's hand in the crook of his arm.

This is how it should be, he thought, *A bright day, money in my pocket, Clara on my arm, visiting mum. All is well.*

Clara's conversation was still fixed upon how horrific the school uniform was. How, perhaps, she could work with Felicity to create a girls' uniform in some nicer colours and a more contemporary style. When she said "contemporary", Peter could only assume that she meant corseted and with dozens of skirts like his mother's female clientele generally preferred.

"Don't you think that younger girls might like the freedom of pants so they can climb trees, or run and play, or do horse riding? I don't think I'd have worked out my magic if I hadn't been in the swamp with the alarm frogs…"

Clara shot him a horrified look. "You want to train girls by making them play in a swamp? Are you trying to destroy their chances of success in polite society?"

Peter frowned. "They're going to be mages, not princesses. They don't need to simper or learn embroidery or find a 'proper' husband. Didn't you ever just want to be free of…" He thought for the right word, then just pointed to the wide skirt, "…that?"

"What, my clothing? No. I like my dresses. This is a little

heavier than what I'm used to but it's nice. It's pretty. It's what girls wear."

"Not everywhere though."

"What do you mean, 'not everywhere'?"

"Well, in the Western lands there are women that wear pants. They ride the sand lizards and fight with the men, and the children, girls and boys together, are raised with swords in their hands. I spent some time there when I was 14. We were visiting a mage who travelled with the tribes — the men wear full flowing, rich robes woven from the silk of the sand weaver. Everybody wears scarves across their faces to protect them from the dust storms. They have these enormous tents they carry from one place to the next, and the main job the mage had in the tribe was to draw water from deep underground."

"Fascinating," Clara said, "But they're not here, this isn't the desert, and women wear dresses."

"Speaking of tents," Peter said, "This is mum's place."

A small blackboard stood out on the footpath proclaiming that Diefen's Dresses was just inside. In the time he had been away, Felicity had put a row of pavers out leading to the shopfront entrance and had planted seedlings either side of the path.

"Pretty," said Clara, looking at the embroidered vines on the white tent.

"Yeah. It's really nice inside too."

But as they stepped up the path, the faint sound of voices came from inside, and then a woman backed out of the door, still yelling.

"...and I will not be spending a cent! Same fabric, same style! You will replace my dress at your own expense!"

She turned. Her face was red and blotchy and she was heaving great breaths. But spying them, her face became even uglier.

"That's my dress," she roared, "That's *my dress!* Why do

you have my dress?"

She ran at Clara and grabbed her by the hair, yanking her head back and dragging her across the flowerbed and away from Peter, who was frozen, looking back and forth between the doorway and the woman dragging Clara and yelling.

"You come into my home, steal my new dress, then you have the nerve to *wear* it in *front* of me? It's *mine!*"

Peter stumbled after her, confused. "But Norman gave it to her," he protested weakly. "Stop. You misunderstand."

Clara was yelling "Stop. Stop." But the woman wasn't listening, and with a voice like thunder, Clara yelled "STOP!"

The woman's head jerked backwards, her fingers untangling from Clara's hair as if they were being directed by a puppeteer. Clara started to glow, a warm, yellow glow in the sunlight, and she looked up at her assailant. The woman was leaning backwards. No, Peter realised, not leaning, she was being pushed backwards. She was being repelled by the glow. She was lifting from the ground and being pushed backwards, out onto the road, falling onto her back. The look on her face had changed from anger to fear as Clara rose to her feet and towered over her.

"This is my dress," Clara said in a low voice.

"Actually, it's not." Felicity's voice demanded attention, and they all looked to where her form had emerged from the doorway. "I finished sewing it three days ago. I would know it anywhere. I don't know who you are or where you got the dress, but it belongs to Vanadine there."

"But Norman gave it to her, mum," Peter pleaded. "Clara doesn't have anything else to wear."

"Then Norman's a thief, plain and simple. I'm sure Vanadine will be civilised about getting the dress back tomorrow, but your friend can't keep it."

The woman Felicity had called Vanadine was nodding fearfully. "T…Tomorrow. Tomorrow's fine. Just don't hurt me."

Clara looked back at the woman, who flinched at her gaze. "I'll bring the dress here, tomorrow, cleaned. You can pick it up then."

Vanadine nodded, crawling backwards, and then stood and ran.

Felicity watched Vanadine's form retreating, then she turned to her son. "You'd better come inside, both of you, and we'll sort out a replacement outfit."

Inside, with a cup of tea between his hands, Peter started shaking. "I told them you were special," he said. "I knew you were special."

"Of course I'm special," Clara protested from the pedestal where she was getting a display dress fitted and hemmed. "I don't need to be a mage to be special, and I'm a bit offended that you think I'm only special now. I don't even think it was me doing that stuff. It didn't feel like it was me."

"Who else could it be," he asked, exasperated. "It wasn't me. I'm pretty sure it wasn't mum. I don't think that woman did it to herself. And this child," he pointed at Yslt, who was playing with some bobbins as if they were toy people, "probably has no idea what's going on."

"I don't know who it was, it just wasn't me," Clara repeated, stepping down from the pedestal to look at the pastel pink gown in the mirror. It was less elaborate than Vanadine's stolen dress, a single colour with no trim or embroidery, and fewer skirts or frills, but it was clean and she was comfortable that this dress was not going to lead to hair pulling this time. "Can I organise five of these, all in different colours? I don't think I need anything for special occasions yet, but these are serviceable for daily use. Perhaps an embroidered apron to make them fancier if I need?"

"If you didn't have clothing, do you have enough money to pay for five? I can't afford to take a loss on that much linen."

"Oh," Clara reached into the embroidered pocket that was slung across a seat and pulled out a chunk of iron. "I don't have any currency, but I have metal. It's pure iron. I got Misty... wait, you know who Misty is, right?" Felicity nodded. "I got Misty to melt it down, and I gave her a taste. She says it's pure. You can check with her if you want."

Felicity looked across at her son, who nodded.

"I'll trust you. Metal, not currency." Felicity sighed, storing the lump in a box. "Okay. It's not ideal, but I can help you out. I'll set up an account for you and I'll keep a total. The smith likes me, I think, and will give me a fair exchange. Now go change so I can get this dress altered. You'll need it tonight if you're dropping the other back off to me tomorrow."

Clara disappeared into the change room.

Moments later, a voice played, sounding like it was coming from everywhere and nowhere.

"This is Magus Norman Linter, addressing the communities of Varthien. I declare that it is now illegal to kill other intelligent creatures for the purpose of eating them. This includes humans, chirren, and alver. It is illegal to consume the meat of an intelligent creature, except for funerary purposes as determined by the direct community of the deceased.

"I declare that pyksees are a danger to the wider population. All known pyksee colonies must be eradicated.

"I declare that any individual involved in kidnap for the purpose of ransom is to be publicly executed.

"That is all."

But they barely noticed as Norman's voice spoke about kidnap and ransom, because the sound of Clara's distress overrode all else and Peter and Felicity ran into the changing room. Clara was face down and squealing on the floor. A large tear in the back of her sleeve revealed a deep gash in her arm and a bloody mark on the fabric. She rocked back and forth, bringing her arm toward her chest as if to protect something.

"What happened?" Peter shouted.

Felicity rushed forward to see to Clara's injury, but the girl scuttled further away, still protecting something close to her chest.

"Don't hurt her, don't hurt her," Clara was muttering. "It's not her fault, don't hurt her."

"Don't hurt who," Peter asked. "There's nobody here."

"It's earlier than planned. Don't hurt her, she didn't mean to. We need to see Norman. We need to go right now."

"I can teleport us," Peter suggested. "We can get there in seconds."

"You need to know, before we go. It's not just me. It's both of us."

"Both? Who, you and mum?"

"No," Clara whispered as she opened her hands slightly. A warm, yellow glow shone from them as a large spider-like creature peeped out of her fingers. "Me and her."

Scaramond was alone when they reached the tower.

"Where's Norman," Peter asked. "So much happened. Clara has magic, and Norman stole Clara's dress, and there's a..."

"Norman's not here. I think it was Bellamy. The magic seemed like his. He likes to pull, that one. I hadn't thought of securing against pulls. Most people push, see? They arrive, they visit, they don't summon people to their presence. He'd make a good war mage, that one, if only he wasn't so caught up on a dead man's philosophies. You said Norman stole the dress? That's not a surprise, but I did think he had more sense than to take it from a local."

Clara's body started glowing. "Where has the Magus gone," she asked with an unfamiliar tone.

Scaramond looked at the glowing girl with shock. "How are you doing that?"

"We need to converse. Where has the Magus gone?"

"You have no magic. How are you doing that?"

"We have pacts that the Magus has broken. Where has the

Magus gone?"

Scaramond looked unnerved. "Who are you," he asked.

"I was about to tell you," said Peter, but was interrupted by the eerie tone spilling from Clara's lips. The large, spiderlike pyksee parted the thick hair on Clara's shoulder to reveal itself. It looked different to other pyksees — its middle sets of limbs were frilled rather than bearing functional wings, and its abdomen was large, swollen, dragging behind it, but it was still indisputably a pyksee.

Clara's voice droned on. "We are the colonies. This Clara is our vessel. She is our ambassador. She is our voice. Where has the Magus gone?"

Scaramond directed his attention to the tiny presence. "Knowing Bellamy, he'll be somewhere in Marthune. Probably the Capital. I think they're calling it Merethien these days. I couldn't swear to that, of course. By the way, is Clara still in there?"

"Of course I'm here," Clara said, her voice suddenly normal again. "The Pyksee are talking through my voice box. Neat, huh?"

The look on Scaramond's face implied that it was anything other than neat.

Peter sighed at the imprecision of Norman's location. "Maybe it would be better if we waited at Norman's tower. I think he may have just declared war on the pyksees."

Chapter 29

Merethien

"This is unacceptable." Bellamy's face was beyond red, almost magenta in his anger. Norman hadn't imagined that the normally gentle man could shout as loudly as he had over the past few minutes.

"You are a Highmage before you are Magus. You are sworn to act without bias or political intent. And yet here we have this fool of a king striding through Qoth claiming the Magus at his back like you're some army! And what's this damned proclamation? You can't enforce laws on common people! You're spitting on the memory of the great Barduce!"

Norman's eyebrows rose at that. "The great Barduce? Do you know what I found when I opened up the succession box and looked at the selection criteria? I don't think anyone's looked at them since his time, as they're written in Ancient Yurdelt. Number one on that list—'completely loyal to Argentus Barduce'. Number two on that list—'sets aside ethical considerations in favour of those determined by Argentus Barduce'. Number three—'no ambition to rise above their station'. Do I need to go on? There are roughly seventy points on this list, and I think they're all pretty much rubbish. What are we doing here? Are we doing what we swore, to work in the best interests of the people of Varthien, or are we holding on to outdated principles that worked only to further the interests of one long-dead man?

"And have you read some of the work of Barduce's contemporaries? The ones that called him a tyrant? A monster? He separated children from their families so he could indoctrinate them! He killed anyone who spoke out publicly against him! Have we learned nothing in five thousand years?"

Bellamy's eyes were bulging and he was huffing in short breaths. His face had taken on an even darker hue, as if all the blood in his body had been squeezed into his head by the tension that radiated from him.

"You spit on the memory of the greatest man to have ever lived! He was kind, virtuous, humble…"

"…murderous, psychotic, sociopathic. You've been taught to believe good things about him. In fact, you've been selected because of those beliefs. And now, I'm changing the selection criteria. They need to be fair. They need to be balanced. They need to allow different thoughts and ideas to emerge without all this apoplexy."

Norman turned his back on Bellamy and casually sat on the embroidered sofa. "It's one of the powers granted as Magus, apparently. I can unilaterally adjust the terms of selection, and I'm surprised it's never been done before. I can unilaterally decide on changes to instruction we give to the populace. We do that already every time we name the new year, but I guess all of the other proclamations just fell by the wayside over time; it seems it was in frequent use in the time of Barduce, then fewer and fewer, until by the time Daraskell came around it was barely in use at all."

Bellamy's face was starting to return to its customary pink now that Norman had taken a less aggressive posture, and his breathing had slowed.

"The Council has always been about laws for mages," he said quietly. "Humans have been considered to be separate jurisdiction…"

"Looking at the numerous invitations to appear, humans are inviting me into their politics. Not just the humans, the Chirren and the Alven too. You talk about us as if mages were not also human."

"We're not. Not according to the Draconic chroniclers, anyway. We came from elsewhere. Interbred. Stuffed up the planet. Then we put the council together and settled down. Then a war, then Barduce. The rest is pretty quiet. And then you decide to change things."

"Change isn't automatically bad. Chirren made me a part of their clan, then I walked into a heated situation where I was served up Chirren by the humans. The humans had already sworn fealty to me, and I wasn't about to let my subjects eat each other willy nilly, so it's a blanket proclamation.

"As for the war, I'll talk with Hrodolf. He did overstep. I am obligated by my title as Earl to answer to Hrodolf, but the Earl of Sharpstone and the Magus are two different people, even if they are in the one body, and he seems to have conflated the two."

Bellamy looked at Norman, concerned. "Be careful," he said. "Change isn't automatically bad, but that doesn't make it good either. Change causes friction. Friction causes heat. And enough heat can set the world on fire.

"And I want you to consider something. Yes, I was chosen according to that list. I am prideful and I like my comforts. But how did you end up on the Council?"

Chapter 30

MANIPULATIONS

661 OM Tarandeer

Atinien Mountain

Scaramond rose, early as always, and made his way directly to Albert's bedside, a bowl of porridge in hand.

"You should have called me before the boy," he said to the bedridden Magus. "There are things I need to discuss with you. I'm overriding succession."

Albert looked up at Scaramond. "You're able to influence the box? There may be uproar if we just up and announce it."

"Don't worry about the box. I put in an override when I made it."

Albert laughed, his wheezing chuckle turning into a cough. "Of course you did. Why would I imagine otherwise? Who will the lucky new Highmage be?"

Scaramond smiled. "Your boy. Norman. And he won't just be Highmage. You're going to name him Magus."

Albert raised an eyebrow. "Norman? Magus? He's so young. And the pressure—I don't know if he'll stand up under the weight." He sighed. "Very well, I'll name him. He's not without talent. That thing with the death of Theo's apprentice really pushed him to internalise his triggers.

"Now, that speech of mine, I know it must have grated. It wasn't too difficult to hear, I hope?"

"I've heard many such speeches before, young man, and I will hear them again. Harder to handle when I was younger, I think. Each of our gifts bears its own cross, and this is mine."

"He'll need support, you know. I hope you'll help him. His views may not be…" a fit of coughing interrupted Albert, and Scaramond waited patiently for it to end. "Change. He'll bring change."

"It's nothing I won't have seen before. There is very little I haven't seen. He'll have my support, if he'll take it. I don't think he likes me much. However, I am rather relying on change. I hope he turns the planet upside down and shakes it. It's time."

"Why now, if it's not an impertinent question?"

"Have you met his apprentice? I think that child has formed the first dragon bond in roughly eight thousand years. The signs are all there. Impressively, they did it with no guidance. They need a world that can change to include them. Norman can give them that."

Albert nodded. "I almost wish I'd be there to see that." He gestured to the bowl beside him. "Better hand me that. He'll be on my case if I don't eat something."

Chapter 31

1 OM Linter

Qoth

Lance Titingarn was just starting up the side of a mountain when the message from the Magus played. He listened with interest to the first proclamation, tutted in annoyance at the second, then sighed heavily at the last.

"What does that mean, sir," Jak asked.

Lance looked over his shoulder at the boy, who was still looking rather uncertain on the back of the large horse. "It means a few things. First, it means we've got a Magus who is going to be a lot more intrusive than the last one. Second, it means that some people are going to be unhappy because their diet needs to change. That doesn't affect me or you, unless you're in the habit of eating people. Third, he wants us to do pest management in the middle of a war. That's annoying but won't break us. And fourth, he would rather we kill certain criminals rather than try to rehabilitate them. People who kidnap for ransom are sometimes just desperate. Poverty makes it seem like they have no real options except to make rich people give it to them.

"There are always options. I want you to remember that. No situation is so dire that you need to take the life of a bystander simply for money."

Jak looked confused. "But don't they give the kidnapped person back afterwards? That isn't taking life."

"What do you think happens if they can't pay?"

"I don't know," said Jak. "What happens?"

"Look at it from the perspective of the kidnapper. If you say you're going to kill someone if you don't get money, and then you don't get paid, it's bad business to let that person go. They might be able to identify you, and the chances of getting paid the next time you try it decrease because people think you might not follow through.

"This means that those people die if there's no payment. And that's not all, sometimes it's easier to kill the victim even if the money comes through.

"I have no problem executing people who willingly hurt and kill other people, but it needs to be a case-by-case basis. Not every kidnapper is the same, and not every punishment should be the same. Some people just need to learn better ways to make money, whereas others like hurting people and will do it again anyway because they enjoy the power. What do you think?"

"I don't know. I used to think that it was all easy to figure out, but I don't think it is anymore." Jak fell silent, and Lance could see that he was thinking hard about the situations posed.

Lance was growing to like the boy. He suspected that the bullying had stemmed from a deeper issue in the home, and that removing the child from that environment had allowed Jak to see wider perspectives. Time would tell. But for the immediate future, there was a four-hour trek up the winding mountain road.

Lord Bogdan Orloff lived in the fortified tower at the top of the mountain. One of Lance's closest neighbours, they had a friendly relationship that had lasted the better part of two decades.

Bogdan met him at the gate, as usual. It's hard to keep your approach a secret when there's nowhere to hide, which was a large part of the tower's defense strategy. No trees, no rocks, just a long, winding road that was completely visible from the tower ramparts for more than two kilometres. A younger Lance used to wonder if all the loose rubble had gone towards making the tower walls. Older now, Lance knew that not only had this assumption been correct, but also that the trees once shrouding the top of the mountain had become the living quarters inside, and had become the bows and arrows that defended it, and furniture, wagons, firewood, and anything left had been sold.

As usual, Bogdan waited for Lance to dismount and greet him with wide arms before stepping forward. It was one of their many rituals — Bogdan was a cautious man and liked to see both hands empty before greeting someone as a friend.

"And who is this you have in tow," he asked in his booming voice. Lance was always certain that Bogdan's voice could be heard all the way to the bottom of the mountain, especially with no trees to block the sound. "Have you been pre-emptively rescuing future criminals again?"

"Nothing pre-emptive about it this time. He was shaking down someone else in my militia. This is Jak. Jak, this is Lord Bogdan Orloff. Dismount and bow when meeting a noble for the first time." The two watched and laughed at the sight of the boy unsteadily dismounted from a horse that was at least five hands too tall for him.

"You need to teach this runt to grow faster," Bogdan said in a stage whisper that was no quieter than his normal voice. "Then he might learn how to get on and off a horse."

The two laughed again as Jak gave an awkward bow.

"That'll do, boy," boomed Bogdan. "You'll do. Treat your Lord well, he'll give you a good start. He'll do you better than most. Better than I would, even. Work to deserve it." He turned to Lance.

"Come in, come in. Standing in the wind is not conducive to talk or hospitality."

Lord Bogdan organised for servants to assist Jak in

unloading the horses and prepare a room for the two guests, then ushered Lance to an empty drinking hall and tapped a keg of mead. "Get that in your belly. A good drop for a cold mountaintop. So, what can I do for Titingarn? It's not often you take on the climb."

Folding himself onto one of the long bench-seats, Lance gratefully took the tankard and had a sip. The mead was both sweet and tart, flavoured with honey and a mix of unfamiliar spices. "The war. What else?"

Bogdan grunted and took a long pull of the tankard, waiting for Lance to expound.

"Hrodolf has entered the field to the northwest and carries my colours. I was trying to stay out of it, give my people as much stability as possible, but it looks like that's not an option any longer."

Bogdan nodded and took another long drink, emptying his cup. "Well." He sighed and rubbed his face as he thought. Then he sighed again and spoke.

"I'll gather troops. We'll bear your colours. Truth be told, you're a better lot for the crown than those cousins of yours, and you may find a good deal of support from unexpected quarters. My opinion of Hrodolf has been raised by this news—I thought he was just an idiot in a shiny hat, but maybe there's actually something of substance in there. You will, of course, stay the evening. It's too late to make your way down the slope now, unless you choose to go down the fast way."

"The fast way?"

"There's a sheer face on the other side. It makes me much less concerned about giving my prisoners windows for fresh air. Some of them choose the fast way down, but few survive it."

Lance chuckled quietly. "I think I'll take you up on your hospitality. And while we're at it, can we take Jak on a tour of your prisons? It might give him an interesting view on the criminal lifestyle."

The evening meal was eaten in the drinking hall, everyone mingling together and serving themselves from a large buffet table, Lord Orloff and Lord Titingarn included. The meal was simple—root vegetables, bread, cheese, and a small amount of meat.

"A rare treat, this," Bogdan said, elbowing Jak in the ribs. "We slaughtered a pig in your honour. Well, not yours, but your patron there. Not often we get guests. Might even soak some bread in the dripping as a nice change for the hollows. You'll get to see those in a little while. So eat hearty. Everybody in this room appreciates your presence, if only for the meat."

After eating, Lance and Bogdan escorted Jak down a long series of tunnels which seemed to branch frequently, and which wound up and around the fortress. Occasionally they would glimpse the outside through narrow arrow slits, bright moonlight flooding the tunnel. Finally, they reached a heavy wooden door. Jak peered off into the darkness to see more doors further down in the tunnel, all on the northern wall.

Bogdan slid aside a small panel in the door and peered through. "Looks empty. Yoo-hoo," he called, "Is there anyone in there?"

A count of three was enough to convince Bogdan that the room was empty, so he lifted the heavy plank that secured the door and swung it open.

"Welcome to the hollows!"

The room was indeed empty but calling it a room was generous. It was more correct to call it an unfenced balcony. It was wide enough and deep enough to give a person room to move, room to sleep, but there was no protection from the elements and the wind buffeted them fiercely. Jak stepped forward to peer off the edge, then hurried to step back—the edge was sheer and in the moonlight it appeared to disappear into nothingness.

"This is where we keep our criminals while they are waiting for trial. If we decide to keep them alive, they often end up back here. There are hollows above us, and below us, and reaching out all the way along the northern face. What do you think, boy?"

But Jak was staring off into the distance. "What's that?" he asked, pointing.

Lance looked out to the horizon, trying to see what Jak had seen. "Can you get rid of the torch," he asked Bogdan, hoping to get a clearer view of the night, and Bogdan complied, stashing the torch in the hall and pulling the door mostly closed. Within moments, Lance's vision cleared. The sky blazed with stars, bright white pinpricks against the deepest navy blue of the night, but they were echoed in yellow across the land. The tiny pinpricks were everywhere, and moving. As he watched, they were coming together in small streams of light, then together into rivers, then more and more until there were huge ribbons of yellow filling the land.

"Insurgents?" Bogdan asked. "That's a lot of torches."

"It looks the wrong colour though. Torches would be more orange, I think. And how can there be that many attackers at once?"

Hrodolf's snores echoed through camp. One tent away, Farrar quietly prayed that the Regent would stop breathing in his sleep; then he might get a full night. He rolled out of his rope bed and put on some slippers. Dressed only in his night-clothes, he stepped out, hoping that the mess still had a little stew in the bottom of the pot.

He only got a few steps before a frantic guard ran up to him.

"We need to flee, sir!" the man said. "The fern-women are upon us!"

"The fern-women?" The guard's dialect marked the man as being from far Eastern Karasta, and Farrar knew that there were some strange legends in some of the more remote steadings. "What are the fern-women?"

"They lie waiting in the ferns, sir, and they lure men and women into their world to live there forever, sir. They've come to take us all!"

Farrar was still confused, but knew that panic like this could spread if there was no strong leadership. "Thank you, man. Show me where they were first spotted and I will deal with the issue."

The man nodded, a relieved expression on his face.

"Thank you, sir. This way."

And so it was that Farrar Angmeyer came to stand at the edge of the camp, watching as endless streams of glowing creatures, looking like a strange cross between dragonflies and women, parted to flow around the camp and then further into the northwest. None of them stopped or entered the camp. Indeed, they were upon them, but they didn't appear to be attacking, or even noticing them.

"Your 'fern-women' appear to be pyksees, man."

"Pyksees? Do we need to 'radicate them now like the Magus says?"

"No, soldier. Stand down. We don't need to eradicate them because they're not posing us an immediate threat. Monitor the situation. If the situation changes, check with me for further instruction.

Farrar looked out at the flow of pyksees. They seemed to be moving with a singular purpose, never stopping, never slowing, brightening the night to an almost painful glow.

Chapter 32

Bakar

Scaramond paced the halls of the empty school, tracing its pathways as he traced the lanes of memory. Had he forgotten them? Had he once known this vital information and thrown it away carelessly? His heartbeat was pounding in his ears, and he found himself nearly running down the halls. He could feel Orange Skies tumbling against the walls of her molten cage, but for once he was more concerned with his own distress than hers, and together they fed each other's turmoil.

Where did the magic come from? He couldn't feel it. He had probed that tiny form with every glimpse of sight he knew and still there was no change; just the background haze of the planet. The link between Clara and the pyksee was invisible. How could he fail after all this time?

He travelled from building to building, searching blindly for answers to his failure, and after an age of fruitless deliberations he found that his feet had brought him to Misty's cave.

"Misty," he called, stopping at the entrance. "Are you available for a consult?"

"Enter," her melodic voice replied from somewhere deep in the cave, and he parted the curtains and stepped into her home.

Scaramond felt pride in the embellishments he had

provided for the injured dragon. The deep carpets and wall hangings had been stored in stasis for too long, and it was good to see them being put to use once more. The small joy cut into the unsettled feeling within him and he felt the roar of his heartbeat quieten, just a little.

"How may I be of assistance, Scarred One?" The voice echoed about the room and Scaramond could not say which side entrance the voice was coming from.

The use of his title was another small joy. Dialectic changes over millennia had altered it beyond meaning into his current name, and it was nice to consider that this was not the only name he had ever carried.

"Do you carry stories of the pyksees within your hoard, Shining One? I find myself at a loss to explain the events of the day."

Misty's golden head pushed through a curtained doorway. She unhurriedly found herself a spot within the cushions scattered around, drawing them into a pile to rest herself on.

"Pull up a cushion, Scarred One, and I will share my stories with you."

"In the time when the World Mirror still stood, Kerathna World-Jumper was named the first Magus, as she had led dragon and Mageunt both to this fertile place. And in that time, it was revealed that the World Mirror had brought us to a place that was not devoid of speaking peoples.

"Kerathna World-Jumper was distressed, for the peoples of this new land lived in harmony and had harnessed the power of steam, which required the metals so cherished by Dragonkind.

"And so it was that she called together the speaking peoples of this new place. And there came before her representatives of each kind—Humanish, those ones so similar to our own Mageunt; the furred Ælven hunters who lived in the treetops and carried their young within pockets upon their bellies; the armoured Chiron who traced the coastlines and owned the seas;

and the Pick-Seers, whose voices were carried through the air and could only be heard through the breath of another.

"And all the peoples bowed to the Pick-Seers, for these tiny ones held the histories of all others, and their blessing brought great wisdom and knowledge. The blessing of the Pick-Seer was so sought after that the peoples would volunteer themselves for trial, even knowing that those found unworthy would be drained of their essential vitality.

"Kerathna World-Jumper sat with the peoples for many days, from the fullness of one moon to the fullness of the next, and together they discussed what it was for dragon and Mageunt to join with their numbers. And Kerathna was sore distressed, for she saw that there would be no easy peace.

"The Pick-Seers were the ones to offer a compromise for all peoples, which would diminish all but would allow all to coexist. And the peoples must forgo warring against each other, and the Humanish must not hoard the metals of their steam devices, and the Ælven must live apart from other peoples and eat only the meat of dumb beasts, and the Chiron must allow settlement along the land's edge that others may farm the oceans, and the Dragon and the Mageunt must destroy the World Mirror that others of their kind might not follow.

"The Pick-Seers would serve to carry the memory of the truce between all, for theirs was a memory that surpassed the individual and was carried by all of their number. And they agreed to reduce their numbers, to reduce their blessings to the peoples that they might govern themselves and to only feed upon those they needed to rather than all who came, for Mageunt were unable to hear the voice of the Pick-Seers or take of their blessing. They valued every individual and each loss would diminish the knowledge of their people. And at each passing of the Magus, the Pick-Seers would choose a vessel for their voice, who would come before the Magus and reaffirm the truce of the peoples.

"Here ends the tale of the First People's Truce, as originally intoned by *Asteroid Rock Tastes of Star Stuff*, bond-mate to Kerathna World-Jumper and carried through the story hoard."

A silence settled over the two, Misty listening to the silence of the cave and Scaramond considering the implications of everything he had just heard. A great, bubbling wall of anger rose in him at the realisation that there were decisions about the fate of his kind that had been kept from him; his careful curation of the line of Magus was undermined by knowledge that had been withheld from him for so long. It was a betrayal that stretched back to the first moments upon this planet, and that had caused his separation from Orange Skies. His distress travelled their bond and his counterpart threw herself again and again into the walls of the magma pocket deep below ground. Scaramond imagined that he could feel the ground shake with her every movement.

"Would you join us, Silent One?"

Misty's voice snapped Scaramond out of his internal rage and he looked up. Chance was stepping through the curtains. The boy nodded a head respectfully at Scaramond, but was that a sly pinch of a smile he noticed, or just another figment? Scaramond thought back and could not say for certain what Chance thought of him or of the world. The boy was a mystery. Was he going to betray Scaramond too, just as Kerathna had done? Just as every Magus since had done?

Chapter 33

THE TASTE OF STONE

Norman's Tower

The bitterness had been growing all day and now was so all pervasive that Suzie barely noticed the sweet splash of teleportation into the area. But it was definitely there, downstairs, outside. The flavour of a mage.

She explored the taste. It had a familiar tang but she couldn't quite place it. Like something she had a hint of in the past but was now more abundant. It wasn't Norman, so it was an intruder, so needed investigation. Suzie stood, wishing the bitterness would subside. It made her feel slow, muddy.

She wished Norman would come home. He had been away much longer than she had anticipated, and wading through this bitter fug made her want to find a refuge and sleep. She had tasted this before, in the wilds, before Norman, when she had wandered in search of a mage. It had existed in the lonely places, hiding in trees and bushes, alive and watchful, flitting from place to place. But never in this sickening pall that covered her. This was a magic she thought might poison her, and she dreaded the thought of being engulfed by this flavour forevermore.

Step by careful step she made her way down the stairs, towards the door on the bottom floor. As she moved, she considered the flavour of the tower seeping through her feet — there was Norman's distinctive magic that had moved the building and held it into this place, but still the flavour of the boy who had shored up its crumbling walls, reinforced the gaps. He was gone, but his magic remained as strong as it was when he had left. It was only ever a hint of flavour, but it was sticky, sweet. It remained.

That was it. The strong splash of sweetness. It was the boy. Peter.

Suzie opened the door. There, indeed, was the boy. Petunia bobbed beside him. Had she grown? Quite sizeably, as she did every time she was with Scaramond, but this growth spurt was very noticeable. And beside Petunia stood a human. Pure, by the taste of it. No, not pure. Hints of that bitterness lay about her. And in the girl's hands, that bitterness was strong. Suzie glared at the pyksee the girl held. Was this why she felt like every step was poison?

But no.

The woods were brighter than normal. They were bathed in the horrible taste, and tiny points of light surrounded the grounds.

"Hello, Suzie," said Peter. "I'm just going to wait for Norman in the dining room."

Well, that's not going to happen, thought Suzie. The boy didn't belong here anymore, so he couldn't just walk in any time he wanted. Suzie stepped outside, shutting the door firmly behind her with her tail, and lay down.

It was distressing to be outside. At least inside there was the comforting taste of magic in the walls, and there were books she could read to distract herself from this nasty flavour, but Norman left her to be guardian, so guardian she was.

Peter approached. There was a frown on his face.

"Shift, Suzie, I can't get past you. You're too big."

Inwardly, Suzie laughed. He didn't get it. He was still in the mindset that he lived here. He didn't see Norman's grief of being abandoned at the biggest and most emotional point in the mage's life. He didn't witness the overwhelming pressures of suddenly receiving hundreds of simpering messages, all begging an audience with fame. He didn't comfort Norman as the new Magus cried for the loss of a father-figure. The boy could rot, for all she cared.

"I don't think Suzie wants us to come in," said Petunia. "We don't live here anymore, remember?"

As usual, the dragon is the perceptive one of the pair, thought Suzie. *Too bad she's shackled to the boy.*

As Peter shoved Suzie with futility, Suzie noticed what was happening with the girl. While Peter and Petunia were distracted, those bitter lights were carrying sticks, twigs, leaves, flowers toward her, building a chair. The tiny sticks were woven together by tiny, nimble hands. The structure looked firm, stable. Even regal. The seat was padded with leaves and flowers, and the girl sat, depositing her charge into a smaller seat woven into the high back. The two sat, the winged pyksee and the girl, and Suzie could taste the acrid waft that engulfed the girl's head. How could the girl stand it?

Peter was kicking her now, with Petunia's vocal objections playing behind him. Just like the boy. It was like he and the dragon would switch. Sometimes he was the careful one, and Petunia would be impetuous and headstrong; at other times, like today, he would take a turn to be irrational and she would become the voice of reason. Someday, Suzie considered, Petunia would be big enough to make a difference to the boy. For now, however, he needed a little extra reminder that caution was advisable in some situations.

She moved her foot slightly and caught his toes between the floor and her stone bulk.

"Aagh!"

He stumbled on his single mobile foot, hopping to stay upright, but failing, falling across her body.

"Let me up, you stupid stone cat!"

That's not the way to talk to someone, thought Suzie.

"Don't call Suzie stupid. You were kicking her. That's not

nice. She didn't do anything to you. You need to apologise. Suzie's our friend. Friends don't kick other friends."

Petunia. Voice of reason. Peter could use some of her childish enthusiasm. He used to have that. He used to question everything and be more about learning things. Then he went through the change. That strange mage thing where they become moody teenagers. The hair on his face corresponded with anger in his heart, Suzie had observed. She hoped he would grow out of it.

A long minute passed, the boy trapped, sprawled across Suzie's back, Petunia voicing her concern and insisting on apologies. Suzie could taste the sweet magic soaking into her directly from the boy. She didn't mind this part of it—her deliberate pettiness was rewarded with his unconscious effort. That flavour was more complex than she had realised while he lived here. Notes of tangy sourness played within the sweet, giving his magic a uniqueness that rivalled only Scaramond's.

When the boy murmured "I'm sorry," into Suzie's stone back, she was almost sorry to release his toes. The strength of his magic so close to her had provided an offset to the flavours of the wild, almost making the bitterness pleasant.

Peter found things to do. He pottered around the garden, tidying things that didn't need tidying, tending and weeding the garden that Norman mostly ignored, chopping wood that Norman probably wouldn't need chopped. Petunia followed him around, giving commentary on everything. And the girl that had accompanied them remained unintroduced, sitting on a throne that had been expanded to a shaded seating nook, seemingly immersed in silent contemplation of the odd-looking pyksee beside her.

Chapter 34

Norman's Tower

It was late afternoon before Norman was able to make it away from Bellamy's seat in Merethien, and he teleported home for the first time in weeks, only to be greeted with the darkness of night. It was a shock to the system, and he froze in confusion for many moments before he recalled that the planet rotated, and that the island continent far to the West was seeing light that had already passed from Arac's skies.

He headed downstairs to find Suzie. Perhaps she would have thoughts about the question that bounced around his skull—the same question Bellamy had posed—how he had been named Highmage when the instructions to the succession box were so contrary to his own experience.

The bright skies outside the small window made the second floor glow eerily, stark orange highlights against the deep black shadows. He glanced briefly out the window, wondering if there had been a volcanic event further East along the range. It was rare, but not unheard of—some deep engine far below Arac's surface kept these mountains alive where others in the arc lay dormant. He didn't recall a full moon, but the disruption of the past weeks could have made him lose track, he supposed.

The view out the window disabused him of these musings, though. Far from dust clogging the skies, clouding the moon, the skies were clear. The forests, however, were lit with tiny embers of orange-yellow light in such numbers that it washed a glow across everything. They traced each tree, each branch, creating skeletal outlines that would normally only be exposed in the heart of winter, far from the late spring foliage that clothed nature now.

There, in the yard surrounding the tower, lay a new structure, tall and thin, lit brighter than the forests as if each speck of light were lined up close together to cover the surface. Beside the structure lay a body curled in the foetal position.

The stairs from the second floor to the first barely registered in Norman's mind as he ran. The door seemed to open of its own accord as he passed the still form of Suzie, ignoring the structure, running for the still form lying on the ground. Then, as he approached Peter, a loud snore broke the night's unnerving silence, and he let out a nervous laugh.

"Oh, thank the gods, you're alive," he heard coming from his mouth, and he sat untidily on the dewy grass. "I thought for sure you were dead."

He was answered with another loud snore from the sleeping Peter, accompanied by a tinier snore in syncopated rhythm from Petunia, tucked up beside Peter's belly.

He slowed his panicked breathing, waiting for his heart to quiet its laboured thumping in his throat, then looked up to inspect the box beside him.

"We have awaited you," a strange voice said from within the box.

Norman tried to see who it was, but the brightness of the outer edge of the box was too much, the darkness within the box too deep.

Closer now than before, however, he could see that the brightness was caused by pyksees. Thousands of them, crawling over the outside of the box, never stopping. The movement made his eyes feel strange, unfocused, and he closed them, trying to shut out the slightly sick feeling they evoked.

"We were sent to discuss our treaty, but you have already declared war. Now we must discuss terms for the end of hostilities."

"War? I didn't declare war on anyone. Are you talking about Hrodolf?" His mind whirled, wondering who was speaking from the darkness. Was this one of the contenders for the Qoth throne, annoyed at the claims that the Magus was taking sides?

"You have announced our eradication from the planet. We come to remind the Mageunt that we were here before you, and that we relinquished power to offer you a place. Should you wish to continue with hostilities, you will find our power to be still great."

"I'm confused. Who are you? I don't know what you're talking about."

A figure leaned forward from the recesses of the black box, and he saw the dark, curly hair of Clara glinting in the yellow light.

"Clara? What's going on? Is this some strange prank you and Peter cooked up? What's with all the pyksees? I didn't know they could be controlled."

"Clara is our voice, but we are not Clara. We are the Pick Seers. We chose Clara to be our ambassador. Clara does not control us, nor does the Mageunt called Peter. Please, Magus, sit."

A wave of force gently pushed Norman's torso, and suddenly he was sitting in a seat that wasn't there moments ago. His arms fell onto armrests of twigs and leaves, smooth petals lining the areas where his hands lay. Clara sat forward, and in the yellow light he saw a new sort of pyksee sitting on her shoulder.

"Prior to your declaration of war, we wished to speak regarding altering the treaty. We have needs. Before your people came to our lands, we had a deep symbiotic connection to all the peoples of Varthien. We enabled them to speak to each other, and we assisted the humans, especially, to create wonders. Their fingers are very suited to being makers. However, your people needed the resources of this world, so we accommodated you. The treaty devised with Kerathna required that we withdraw, so this is what we did. However, we need humans."

"You eat humans." Disgust covered Norman's face.

"We do. Rarely. When we deem a person's accomplishments to be of sufficient import that they need to be preserved, we take the person into ourselves. We are able to then include every moment of that person's being in our memory. You can see the memory of this process in the funerary rites of the Chirren. We no longer participate in every funeral, as per the treaty, but the Chirren have attempted to carry on the process. Sadly, it is a futile gesture.

"But now, humans are dying out. We need to address this…"

"Humans aren't dying out. We're everywhere!"

"You misunderstand. You are not human. You're part Mageunt. This gives you access to the Mageunt magic, but it makes you unable to share in our gifts. We are unable to take you into ourselves. There is no connection. When we say that humans are dying out, it is because they are being bred with Mageunt. We now estimate that one in 100,000 people are pure human."

"Okay. So what? I can't do anything about that."

"We propose to take an active course in human affairs once more, so that we can begin to rebuild the human population."

"What does that mean? How can you do that?"

"We will build a human breeding program…"

"You propose to force people into some sort of genetic breeding program? That's abhorrent! No matter what, I would never agree to that."

"Ah." The voice sounded sad. "Then your declaration of war is accepted. We will now treat mages as hostile and the treaty is broken."

Chapter 35

Qoth

Looking out towards the yellow river with interest, Lance was astonished to see a stream break off and head into the valley below the mountain. He elbowed Bogdan in the side.

"What do you think that means?"

Bogdan pursed his lips. "Well, I don't know. It's not really a threat on this side…"

He stopped mid-thought as the glow reached the base of the sheer cliff and started to mass below.

"They can't get up here, whatever they are, and they can't dig through the rock. That's pure basalt. Tough as they come."

Jak peered over the edge. "Uh, I think they're coming up here."

"Impossible. There's no way any force could reach the Hollows." He turned away to the door, just as the first points of light reached the edge. Within seconds, both Jak and Lance were surrounded by yellow lights, and they were lifted from the ground to be swathed in strands of silk.

Bogdan turned, his hand on the door, and beheld his companions swinging from the roof, struggling to free themselves. In terror, he pushed through the open door and slammed it shut behind him, dropping the heavy locking bar in place.

Watching the flow of pyksees close up, Farrar had no time to react as they engulfed his form. The lone soldier standing by watched in astonishment for several seconds, then ran to the tent where the King was sleeping. Bursting through the canvas flap, he swallowed heavily as the form of King Hrodolf lay swaddled in a fine, white, silken cocoon.

Chk was communing with Mother Water when the glow of daylight filled the streets of Wamanil. He waded from the water, chelipeds wide and high in the sign of reverence.

"Father Sky, I have awaited your blessing. Join with me in gladness."

He stepped to the Slings of the Father and reclined, rejoicing as the light of Father Sky clothed him in the Shroud of Blessing.

Appendix

OM Fellin (24 years)

Interregnum (4 years)

> (This period is sometimes termed the Interregnum war or the Highmage war)

OM Barduce (973 years)

4 Contract tokens replace school system

The succession box is created

Yslt is abandoned in a stasis field, age 5

OM Jlaskil (526 years)

OM Houn (1438 years)

OM Daraskell (1947 years)

OM Pitchworth (842 years)

OM Tarandeer

1 Albert Tarandeer becomes Magus, age 78

597 Estrella Linter is born

619 Norman Linter is born

621 Gareth Diefen is born

624 Felicity Parnat is born

627 Norman Linter enters the employ of Albert Tarandeer, age 8

637 Norman Linter reaches majority

642 Felicity Parnat weds Gareth Diefen

643 Death of Gareth Diefen

Peter Diefen is born

647 Clara Angmeyer is born

653 Misty enters household of the Cutler family

Petunia is hatched

Peter Diefen enters the employ of Norman Linter,

age 10

661   Misty is rescued from enslavement

OM Linter

1   Death of Albert Tarandeer

        Norman Linter becomes Highmage and Magus, age 44

        Peter Diefen reaches majority

        Clara Angmeyer reaches the Karastan border, age 14

        Yslt is freed from stasis, age 5

CHARACTERS

Abercrombie	A Highmage
Albert Tarandeer	Norman's mentor
	Magus
Alf	Brutish guard at the Karastan border, later a deserter
Artun	Guard at the Karastan border
Asteroid Rock Tastes of Star Stuff	Bond mate to Kerathna World Jumper
Bellamy Foljur	A Highmage
Chance	Scaramond's apprentice
Chk	Chirren of Wamanil clan
Clara Angmeyer	Daughter to General Farrar Angmeyer
Colton	Steward to King Hrodolf of Karasta
Creevy	Guard at the Karastan border
Em	Chirren of the Wamanil clan
Estrella Linter	Norman Linter's mother
Farrar Angmeyer	General in the Karastan army
Felicity Diefen	Peter's mother.
Fig	A deserter from the Karastan army
Gantry	A mage, familiar with stone magic
Gareth Diefen	Mage with architectural focus.
	Peter's father
	Felicity's husband
	Norman's friend
	Apprentice to Theophrastus
Hrodolf	King of Karasta
Jak	Servant to Lance Titingarn

Kerathna World-Jumper	One of the first Mageunt in Varthien
Misty	Dragon — gold
	Full name — The Sun Shines on the Misty Valleys and Burns Away the Shadow
	Petunia's mother
	Enslaved by the Cutler family between 653 — 661 OM Tarandeer
Norman Linter	Mage with scent focus.
	Apprentice to Albert Tarandeer
	Peter's mentor
	Friend to Gareth Diefen
	Highmage Magus
	Earl of Sharpstone
Pat	Lord Titingarn's stable hand
Peter Diefen	Former apprentice to Norman Linter
Petunia	Dragon — red
	Full name — The Blossom of the One Who Offers Life
	Misty's daughter
Reginald Cutler	The butcher's son. Known as a bully in the local Pugton area
Rob	A farmer posing as an Earl, killed at the Karastan border
Russ	A deserter from the Karastan army
Scaramond	Mageunt
	A mage with a pain focus.
	Mentor to Chance
	Also known as Skaraman
	Also known as the Scarred One
Suzie	Gargoyle in the shape of a cat, companion to Norman Linter.

Theophrastus	A Highmage. Shapechanger.
Lance Titingarn	Noble of Qoth, fond of pigeons
Yslt	A child captured in stasis for 5535 years
Nanny Triph	Yslt's nanny
Bogdan Orloff	A local Lord in the southern Qoth region
Vanadine	Felicity Diefen's customer
Vashun	Lord Titingarn's steward

GLOSSARY

Alarm-frogs	Magical frogs that emit piercing shrieks if disturbed
Alven (also Alver, also Ælven)	Intelligent marsupials that inhabit the Northeastern Reaches. The Alven are highly communal and exist in small clans that trade with each other.
Ancient Yurdelt	A language that was current at the time of Argentus Barduce.
Arac	A northern country in the Eastern continent.
Atinien Mountain	A mountain in Varthien's Northern Reach, home to Magus Albert Tarandeer
Bakar	An unwalled town of roughly 10,000 people.
Caisson	A wagon for carrying a coffer
Catafalque	A funeral structure used for lying in of state
Chirren (also Chiron)	Intelligent arthropods. The Chirren are semi-aquatic social creatures that populate littoral zones across most of Varthien.
Cortege	Funeral procession
Delingaard	A country in the south-west of Varthien's Western continent
Delingaard Imperial Palace	Imperial palace of the Delingaard line, a family known for liberal views on slavery and torture.
Fire Starter	A magical device that sets a small twig on fire for the purpose of firing hearths
Gargoyle	A magical creature created from artistic

	inspiration
Garthanian	A forest in the southern part of the Eastern continent, known for a species of tree that can communicate with other living organisms.
Glisterweed	A light-emitting plant found in underground caverns
Guilder	Currency of Karasta
Hedgemage	A person whose magic requires active application of plants or minerals.
Highmage	A mage who has been appointed to the Council of Mages
Hyn	Gender non-specific pronoun. This is a vestige of the language Yslt spoke prior to stasis, which contained no gender-specific terms. Hyn can mean I, me, my, she, her, hers, he, him, his, singular they, singular them, singular their. Plural they, them, their had a different word.
Light-bob	A magical light which can be set to stay in one place or follow a given subject.
Mage	A person who is able to use magic
Mageunt	The species of humanoid that mages are descended from
Magus	The thirteenth member of the Council of Mages, who stands apart from the rest of the council and is the arbiter of disputes. Often seen as the leader of the Council. Can set policy.
Marthune	Island continent South of the Shard Sea
Merethien	Largest city on the Island of Marthune
OM	"Our Magus"; terminology to describe the year, marking from the year of ascension to the year of the Magus stepping down.

	Years where no magus sits are marked as interregnum.
Pell	A structure (often a padded pole) used to practice sword-blows.
Prithant	A planet inhabited by Mageunt before they came to Varthien
Pugton	Birthplace of Peter Diefen. Home of Felicity Diefen.
Pyksee (also Pick-Seer, also Fern Women)	*Archaeidae sapiens.* An arachnid species known for its wings and communal behaviour.
Qoth	An equatorial country located on the western shoreline of the Eastern continent
Rin	Currency of Qoth
Scutage	A tax paid by a landed noble in lieu of military service
Sense Trigger	A focus that enables a mage to cast a spell. Sense triggers differ person to person.
Shattering, The	Specifically, the Shattering of the World Mirror, an event in Varthien's history that caused the World Mirror to explode, which then caused tectonic upheaval throughout Varthien. Over a period of 800 years, Varthien's single continent broke into several land masses, burying or drowning large areas of human habitation in a succession of seismic events and causing long periods of polluted skies from intense volcanic eruptions and fires. Due to the nature of the Shattering, it also caused fracturing of local dimensional spaces, permanently disabling travel to or from the planet.
Sorcerer	A person whose magic requires active application of schematics or mathematics.

Storyhoard	A dragon who collects the stories of other dragons, to pass along to future generations of dragon.
Succession box	In the wake of the sudden death of Magus Fellin and the 4-year interregnum that followed, the succession box was created in 4 OM Barduce by Magus Argentus Barduce to remove issues arising from the death of any Highmage.
Trucent	Currency of Pavane
Varthien	The world in which the events take place
Wamanil	A clan of chirren located in Qoth
Wizard	A mage who has learned to use magic without relying upon a sense trigger
World Mirror	The portal that Draconid and Mageunt forces used to arrive in Varthien
Wyrm	A dragon
Wyrmling	An infant dragon
Yurdelt	Island continent North of the Shard Sea